T0064590

PARKER'S ODYSSEYS AFTER THE APOCALYPSE

BOOK 1

CASEY JOHNSTON

authorHOUSE®

AuthorHouse™ LLC
1663 Liberty Drive
Bloomington, IN 47403
www.authorhouse.com
Phone: 1-800-839-8640

Published by AuthorHouse   03/28/2014

ISBN: 978-1-4918-9999-1 (sc)
ISBN: 978-1-4918-9997-7 (hc)
ISBN: 978-1-4918-9998-4 (e)

Library of Congress Control Number: 2014906052

Contents

Chapter 1—Mountains..1

Chapter 2—The First Meal.. 19

Chapter 3—Fort Montaña..32

Chapter 4—Sam the Rancher 40

Chapter 5—Blue Eyes Blue..52

Chapter 6—The Court-Martial 71

Chapter 7—Time to Do Your Job 79

Chapter 8—Almost Dying Isn't That Bad 95

Chapter 9—To the Hospital.. 117

Chapter 10—Out of the Hospital 131

About the Author.. 141

Chapter 1—Mountains

"I'm climbing the steep face of a barren mountainside. Many events have led me to where I am standing now. Some were terrible and some were decent, but none were as shattering as the outbreak of the most devastating plague mankind has ever experienced. Last I heard, nearly—"

"Mountains . . . why do mountains have to be so damn tall?"

"*Hey!* I'm trying to have a moment of deep reflection. Could you wait until I'm finished?"

I huffed as I put one foot in front of the other on my seemingly endless ascent to the top of the tallest mountain I could find. Actually, it wasn't the tallest, just the most time-consuming and tiring. For the past few days I'd been on the run from some foul-tempered people I'd managed to aggravate.

I looked behind me. No one so far . . . I assumed they gave up the chase. Then again, I assumed they wouldn't shoot me on sight . . . I thought I'd keep climbing.

"What are you, a paranoid cat? Let's go back and see if we can find a mattress. I'm tired of sleeping in the dirt."

I stopped and glared at the dark figure who'd been haunting my steps since my sanity fractured.

"Just because I'm a figment of your imagination doesn't mean I like camping every night."

Sigh. I turned my gaze from the dark, grinning figure and drew in a deep breath to ease the building frustration of putting up with the incorporeal nut job. I took another step, and my thick army boots slipped out from under me.

"Don't get me wrong, I like s'mores just as much as any other guy, but monotony is tiresome."

I frantically grasped the thin weeds around me as I slipped down the steep incline. The gravel fell apart as I desperately tried finding a firm foothold.

The specter looked down at me. "Are you listening?"

I finally found a large rock and stopped my descent. My heart was deafening as it pumped adrenaline through my body. Sweat ran down my face, leaving paths in the dust and dirt on my skin. When I was able to regain control of my breathing, I started climbing again.

I glared at the phantom. "Do you ever stop talking?"

He smiled. "Technically you're talking to yourself."

God, I hate this guy so much. But for now I can't be distracted by things I can't change. The sun was setting and I needed to focus on finding a place to sleep before nightfall.

I clenched my teeth and focused on the thin trail I was using to climb the nearly vertical face. One more misstep could be the difference between reaching the top or falling down the side.

*

By the time I found a promising campsite the sun was nearly touching the horizon. I let out a sigh of relief as my tired legs begged me to sit and rest. Regrettably, I was far from being done for the day. Before I could rest for the night, I needed to survey my surroundings, start a fire, and—my stomach clenched as I noticed a narrow cave around the bend of the mountain. I immediately grabbed my knife and hatchet and struck a defensive position.

The shadowy man raised his eyebrows. "Uh-oh, this looks like a problem!"

I was tempted to say something to my ghostly stalker, but this was really not the time to be distracted. If I was going to stay on this ledge tonight, I needed to make sure I was completely alone.

I ignored him and crept closer. The sun had set enough that the cave was pitch black, so it was difficult for my eyes to adjust. All the while I kept the only weapons I owned, a knife and a hatchet, tensed and ready to strike. My heart pounded as I walked slowly through the narrow opening. A few steps in my hands started to sweat inside my cowhide gloves and my shoulders were uncomfortably compressed as they strained the seams of my long leather coat. I—

Taaannnnggggg!

My arm jolted as the knife in my hand hit the back wall. I froze. The sound wasn't very loud, but in the quiet of this darkness it was deafening. Eventually I came to the conclusion that I was alone and could relax. If there was anything in here I was pretty sure I would know by now.

I let out a sigh of relief and let my arms drop. I walked out of the cave, tossed my weapons into my pack, and prepared a small stone circle to contain my fire. Afterward I'd find some kindling, finally start my fire, and finally relax.

*

Minutes passed and the fire steadily grew. As I relaxed, it occurred to me the sun had set and the night had engulfed the land in darkness and silence—all except for the dancing flames of my fire and the soft crackling of the burning wood.

Before long I was mesmerized by the yellow and orange glow before me and slowly slipped into a trance-like state where memories of the past ran through my mind's eye like a reel from an old film.

Before the end of the world, I'd served as a field surgeon in the US army. I was unlucky enough to be sent to the UK for my virgin tour. It was horrible. Nobody ever guessed that such a beautiful country could ever become such a hole. Then again . . . when a prime minister is shot and schools are bombed, one thing leads to another and a war starts. It certainly didn't help that competing corporations decided to get involved. Their involvement was like gasoline on a bonfire, and it was only a matter of time before everything spun out of control.

I closed my eyes and tried to think of something else.

I reach for my pack and withdrew a whetstone, deciding to start with my knife. I listened to the smooth and nearly silent grind as the stone slid along the length of the steel blade.

I once again slipped deep into thought.

I don't think anyone really knows what happened, but halfway through the first year of war a disease or a pathogen was born. It spread across the world so quickly that no one had time to react. Cities and countries fell, one after the other, as the plague consumed the world. A terrible sickness that turned average humans into—

I jumped as my hand slipped and cut my finger on the edge of my knife. While clenching my teeth and gripping the cut tightly I suppressed a scream of frustration. I hunched over putting pressure on the laceration and breathed heavily.

I really missed my iPod.

When I woke the next morning I pulled my coat and blanket tightly around my shoulders to keep out the brisk morning air. I blinked tiredly and massaged a sore spot on the back of my neck. I kinked my neck and heard a satisfying pop as the bones snapped back into place. I then turned to the smoldering remains of the fire. I stirred them and then turned to my bag and started searching for the last bits of food. I had some deer jerky from a while back.

The figure smirked. "It's already gone."

I shook my head. "No, I had at least another day's worth."

The figure leaned on his knees. "That bag looks pretty empty to me."

Panic gripped my stomach, and I tried not to acknowledge the specter looking over my shoulder. Unfortunately, I never can ignore him for very long, and he was getting really annoying.

I grabbed my knife and lashed out at him. It never does any good, but he backs off.

I snapped at him. "Don't you have something better to do?"

He shrugged. "Not really."

I punched the ground. "Damn! What do I have to do to get rid of you?"

He sat on a rock a little ways away. "Oh, you'll never be rid of me . . . not until you understand why I'm here."

I leapt to my feet and slashed at him again. "Dammit! Who are you?"

He danced just out of reach. "*You created me, so you run away from the past.* If you don't know, then I don't. Look, we've had this conversation before, and every time it ends the same. You get frustrated and then turn and walk away."

I got up and walked away.

He started to clap. "*Yes!* Just like that! *Man,* are we in a rut."

I massaged my eyes. "Whatever . . ."

I shook my head and turned my attention to other things. I'd need to find the necessities for survival if I wanted to stay here, but if I found even one infected creature I was leaving. I wasn't taking any chances.

The creatures were victims of the UK Infection. Popular belief was that the strain had been created by some government corporation to chemically enhance foot soldiers by giving them a focused berserker mindset on the battlefield. Making them stronger, faster, immune to pain, and harder to kill. Obviously something went wrong and led to the death—or something similar to death—of more than eight billion members of the human race. The sickness burned governments and corporations to the ground, leaving the leaderless masses disoriented and unable to stand against the panic, fear, and death. It was just like one of those zombie movies.

The shadowy man smiled. "Wow, you really are in a morbid mood today!"

I ignored him. Time to study the landscape.

I looked out on the vast prairie that I had wandered onto before climbing this mountain. From my lookout I could see no trace of my pursuers. The brisk early morning light cleared the sky of all clouds and allowed me to see the world from a new perspective. The weed-covered hills I tiredly walked across for the past three days took on a golden hue that was made even more beautiful by the sapphire-blue sky. For a moment my heart beat with new vigor.

But as the moments passed I remembered there were other things that needed to be taken care of. I reluctantly turned back to my empty food bag and made to put it and my other things in the cave. But as I approached I noticed something I hadn't seen last night.

The shadow looked over my shoulder. "Hey, that wall is man-made."

As much as I hated to agree with my stalker, he was right. The wall at the back of the cave was man-made. It was made of concrete, and there was even a door-shaped impression. I studied the wall and decided it was too well enforced to pry open. Who knew what was on the other side? The best course of action would be to find the front door and see if I could learn anything.

The specter smiled. "We'll need to explore the mountain anyway."

"Shut up."

It had been half a day and I'd been scouting a trail that started from my ledge and sloped along the face of the mountain. It might lead me to the mouth of a canyon or an old riverbed.

I mused, "Maybe there's some water down th—wait . . . are those train tracks? They *are* . . . and power lines? They're on a ledge halfway up the canyon wall, on the other side."

About an hour or two later, I managed to work my way to the bottom of the cool shade of the canyon floor. The canyon was maybe forty feet wide, five stories tall, and . . . well I couldn't tell how long it was from here. Those tracks were still out of reach, but there appeared to be a trail that led up to it just ahead.

I looked back the way I came and lifted my hat to wipe the sweat from my brow. It was getting late, and I really didn't feel like trying an unsuccessful search for my campsite after dark. Might as well find a place to sleep at the top of the trail and start again in the morning when I had more energy.

*

Through blurry eyes I looked around the old cargo train. It was early morning and I was anxious to get back to sleep. I glanced at the dim light on the tram's dashboard. Maybe the tram still worked. Maybe it could take me to other survivors. Maybe they'd have food . . . or a *real* bed. I lay back on the bench. Then again, maybe they would prefer to greet me with a bullet instead of a meal. I shook my head. *Why am I so damn afraid?*

The figure materialized lying on a bench across from me before sitting up. "Hey! Think quieter, I'm trying to sleep over here. Ah, who am I kidding? As long as you're awake, I'm awake. I like you that much."

I furrowed my brow. "Shut up."

The figure stretched and stood up. "Ooooh. Looks like someone woke up on the wrong side of the bench."

I decided to give up on sleep and walked over to the driver's controls. If I messed with the controls I might be able to get this thing moving. After pushing some buttons, turning dials, and pulling levers I accidentally released the emergency brake. In an instant, the tram lurched forward and started rolling deeper into the canyon.

For a little while I enjoyed a cool night's ride in the dark as the tram weaved through the canyon. The canyon's height changed from wide to narrow and short to tall . . . fifty stories taller. Then the feeling of bliss crashed to a halt as I rounded a corner and saw bright lights and the dark outline of an enormous structure. A cold fear gripped my stomach as I searched for the emergency brake.

It was a stupid mistake to take the tram this far. I had no idea who or what was at the end of the line, and I didn't want to find out so soon, but before I could get to the brake, the tram slowed down on its own. It came to a halt about thirty feet from what looked like a loading platform. I didn't like how the tram stopped on its own. Odds were I'd been had by someone and he or she was gearing up to attack.

What to do, what to do . . . getting out might mean meeting with some unsavory people. Trying to get the tram moving back the way I came might work, and maybe I'd be able to find a spot that I could—

Choom!

With a loud blast, several floodlights turned on and centered on the tram. The ambient light lit the entire canyon. I threw up an arm to protect my eyes, but it was too late. I couldn't see anything but disorienting colors. In moments the sounds of heavy army boots followed by a chorus of cocking firing pins surrounded me.

I was clearly outmatched. I felt for my knife and axe, but they both seemed a little small.

If I want to live, I can't do anything.

Then a voice as loud as the floodlights were bright rang out over a microphone. "Drop any weapons you have and exit the tram now!"

I didn't move. I was still processing what I should do. Then I heard the persuasive sound of at least a dozen big guns aim at me. "Drop your weapons and come out now!"

I realized doing anything else would be a mistake. I could only hope an opportune moment would come along so I could escape.

I walked out the doors and clumsily dropped my weapons on the ground. The formless shapes of at least three men stepped forward into the blinding light. I couldn't make out any distinctive features as my sight was still filled with shifting colors. Everything was still. I heard men breathing heavily over the loud buzzing of the floodlights.

Someone with a Spanish accent spoke. "We are going to frisk you. Take off your coat and put your arms on your head."

I hesitated.

"If you do not do as I say now, we will fire and kill you where you stand."

He made a rather persuasive argument.

I slowly took off my heavy leather coat and raised my arms. Soon after, a man in full riot gear began the routine pat down with a little more force than necessary. When he finished, he secured my arms behind my back with a pair of handcuffs. Finally the man turned and nodded toward the floodlights.

The voice rang out. "*Bueno*. Now that's done, cut the lights!"

With another loud *CHOOM!* the lights went out.

The man spoke again with a heavy Spanish accent. "Sorry for this rude greeting, but being overconfident is dangerous in the world we live in. Please, come this way."

I nodded in the direction of his voice and started to blindly walk forward. My eyes were just about adjusted when the floodlights were cut off, so once again I fell back into a world of electric dots and discolored blobs.

Thankfully, someone grabbed my shoulder and shoved me forward. "Move."

My vision started to return as we reached the steps to the tram's massive loading platform, but it was only after I climbed the stairs that I had the chance to fully appreciate the sight of the impressive wall in front of me. It stood nearly twenty feet tall and was at least fifty feet long. As we walked along the base to a small side entrance, weaker spotlights shined down on each member of the recon party before stopping on me.

The tall man looked up at a security camera and then signaled some unseen guards. A buzzer sounded, and the gates slowly opened to grant us access to a long and well-lit hallway. From here I was better able to examine my captors. Every man wore black or camouflaged army riot armor and carried a standard assault rifle. They stood in a uniform manner, each ready to shoot me.

We continued down several more unmarked hallways before we stopped at a door marked exit 18, where a tall man at the head of the group turned and spoke to the men. "Stevenson, Wesley, Schwartz, Christen—you four come with me to escort our guest. The rest of you may be on your way."

The men nodded and continued down the hallway, heading toward whatever post or bed awaited them. The men who remained kept their rifles trained on me, and we continued through the door to a concrete road and a windowless black van.

I looked at the men. "This is quite an interesting castle you have."

No one said a word except for the tall man. "Ah, you finally speak. I was wondering if you had lost your voice. We will reach our destination momentarily."

It wasn't long until before the van stopped and I was led to an entrance of a building with the sign POLICIA above it. The tall man opened the doors, and I was ushered into a well-lit lobby. In front of us sat a woman behind a receptionist desk. She glanced at me and then began speaking Spanish with my most gracious host. When they were finished, the woman wrote something down, and once again I was escorted further into the POLICIA building.

When we stopped at a metal door, the tall man turned and addressed his men. "Put our guest inside and then retrieve Alexa."

They nodded and shoved me inside the small room. Inside was a table anchored to the floor, several chairs, a bench, and one dim light bulb. I looked back and saw the tall man saunter toward the bench and sit before gesturing to one of the chairs. As I took my seat, I noticed the fourth man walk in behind me and stand in the corner next to the door.

After sitting, I fully examined my captors. The tall man was thick and muscular. His ridiculously big arms, wide chest, and thick neck barely fit inside his already-massive suit of body armor. When he took off his helmet, I could tell he was maybe fifty, sixty at most, and had a few wrinkles that creased along his strong jaw, leading to a smooth, bald head. His only hair was limited to an enormous black mustache that started at his nostrils and flowed smoothly to the corners of his mouth, ending in waxed crescent-upward curls. He reminded me of a nineteenth-century strongman who'd wear leopard skin togas and spend time lifting dumbbells. Instead, he sat opposite me and set his automatic rifle down on the table.

I turned and examined the other man. From what I could tell, he was just around age twenty. His oily hair hug limply over chalk-white skin stretched tightly around his skeletal face. Unlike the man across from me, he was thin and looked weak. He had a smug expression and gave the impression he spent his free time harassing people and listening to death metal.

The bodybuilder cleared his throat and spoke. "My, my, my, tonight has been the most extraordinary night I've had in a long time. Imagine my surprise when I heard our tram was on its way back to us two days ahead of schedule. By the way, my ragged and worn-down friend, I am Diego Cesar Marcos Tadeo Rivera. But the residents call me Diego."

I forced a smile. "Thank you, Mr. Rivera. My name is Scott Parker, but call me Parker. Everyone I ever knew did."

Diego then let out a booming laugh that blew out my eardrums. "Please, please . . . no need for formalities, just call me Diego. Oh, how could I have forgotten? This man in the corner is named Charlie Christen."

I turned to the thin man and nodded. "Good to meet you, Charlie."

Charlie continued to smile with a strong sense of superiority.

Diego cleared his throat.

I turned back to him and smiled. "Well, I am sorry if I ruined your night."

Diego grinned. "I must admit that waking so early in the morning was much easier several years ago. But I was very excited to meet a strange horse without fear at our door. Oh, and I apologize again for the rather rude greeting we gave you, but we cannot invite every stranger into our home without following proper procedure. There are many good people here, and my priority is to protect them. I have to make sure you do not carry the disease."

I nodded. "I understand, but how can you be sure I don't?"

His grin broadened. "I cannot, but my Alexa can. She has an uncanny ability to take care of many diseases, and has the most amazing ability to determine someone's character in a very short time."

Diego seemed very proud of her, and even more proud to be the one introducing her.

I looked toward the door. "Is she the one we're waiting for? Well, do you mind if we hurry? I am very—"

Charlie interrupted. "I don't think you are in any position to be impatient."

I looked at Charlie. His smug attitude was becoming annoying. We locked eyes, and a chill ran up my spine. During an old tour through Africa I managed to lock eyes with a jackal who was trying to scare me away from its meal. Charlie had those same eyes.

I turned back to Diego, who was also looking at Charlie with an annoyed expression.

Diego turned toward me. "Please excuse Charlie. His manners leave much to be desired."

With an eye roll, Charlie turned away and stared at the wall.

To break the tension I tried a joke. "Ironic that *he* is the one accusing me of being impatient."

Diego grinned. "Yes, we are all young at some point . . . and to answer your question, she will be here soon to look at you."

I nodded. "It seems you are quite proud of Alexa."

Diego smiled. "Sí, I am. She's one of the people who help organize this place and has proven time and again to be more courageous and a better fighter than many of my men. The only reason she is not in the—"

Charlie scolded Diego. "You shouldn't tell him so much, Sta—sir." Charlie stopped halfway through his remark at Diego and shrank further into the corner.

Diego was looking even more annoyed.

I looked at Charlie and smiled. "Charlie, I think you need to calm down."

Charlie frowned and continued to stare at the corner. Charlie was obviously starting to dislike me. However, Diego seemed as though he was enjoying my company. He smiled and lightly tugged on his moustache, probably trying to gather his thoughts and remember where we left off. He furrowed his brow and looked at me. "Where were we?"

I smiled. "Your Alexa?"

Remembrance dawned on Diego. "Ahhh, yes, she is—" He was once again interrupted, this time by the guard opening the door. He looked at Diego for a second to get the go-ahead, and when Diego nodded, the guard stepped out. Another second passed and he reemerged with a young woman with a standard medical bag. She looked to be in her early twenties, and even though she wore heavy doctor's coat and loose army pants, I could tell she had a lithe figure. She turned to smile at Diego, and I observed her pitch-black wavy hair, tanned skin, and a certain air of confidence about her, similar to Diego.

Diego smiled back at her. He got up and with his booming voice said, "*¡Ahhh, Alexa! Mi pequeña flor. ¡Qué bueno verte!*"

She replied. "*Abuelo, qué gusto verte. ¿Quién es este?*"

They continued to greet each other in Spanish, and I continued to not understand anything they said, but after formalities, they finally stopped and turned to me.

Diego grinned and gestured toward me. "Mr. Parker, I have the honor to introduce my granddaughter, Alexa Diego Jesus Rivera, also known as the most competent doctor here. Alexa, this is Scott Parker."

Again she smiled. "Mr. Parker, it is very nice to meet you."

I smiled back and gave her a nod. "Likewise, and Parker is just fine."

She pulled up a chair and sat in front of me. "I hope you don't mind, but I'm going to ask you some quick questions and give you a quick look over to determine your health." Alexa's accent wasn't as thick as Diego's but it was still present.

I nodded. "All right."

She put on some surgical gloves and flashed a small light in my eye to examine the pupil and reaction time. "How did you know about this place?"

I looked straight ahead and tried not to blink as the bright light flashed in my eyes. "I was running from guys who wanted me dead and I stumbled upon your back door. After that I decided to explore the mountain, found the tram, and followed the tracks to your front door."

She pulled out a tongue depressor and examined the inside of my mouth and then checked the inside of my ears and eyes with an otoscope. When she was satisfied, she pulled out a pen and notepad. "What have you been doing for the last few years?"

I blinked the light stains from my eyes. "I've been bouncing between survivor settlements."

Then she moved on to the standard examination process of checking pulse, respirations, and blood pressure. "You didn't try to stay at any of them? Why?"

My vision cleared, and I watched her take my pulse. "Various reasons, such as corrupt or zealot governing bodies, the security was too lax and the settlement fell victim to infection, or it was time to move on."

Diego smiled in the background while Alexa made no reaction. "What made you feel like it was time to move on?"

I winced as she stuck a needle in my arm. "Sometimes I was hired to do assassinations, and when I finished, I didn't want to stay for the fallout or the rebuilding."

Diego and Charlie fell silent. Alexa on the other hand continued to draw blood as if I were commenting on the weather. When she finished, she ran it through a small machine in her handbag. "What kind of assassinations?"

I sighed and tried to ignore the cold metal puncturing my skin. "Sometimes I was hired to kill the heads of marauders, bullies, or the corrupt, or overzealous governing bodies."

Alexa pulled the needle out and placed a soft cotton ball over the puncture. "What did you do before the outbreak?"

I put pressure on the ball as she pulled away. "I was a field medic and then a field surgeon."

She placed a bandage over the cotton ball and wrote a few more things on her notepad.

When she finished, she turned to Diego and spoke to him in Spanish with a smile.

Diego grinned and once again laughed, simultaneously blowing out my eardrums and shaking the cell walls. "My friend, after inspection, my granddaughter has made her assessment. You are welcome to stay overnight if desired. Guards, show Mr. Parker where he can wash and put on some decent clothes. In the morning we'll get something for him to eat!"

My stomach twinged when I heard food. "What are the chances I can get some food now?

Diego grinned again. "Ah, but breakfast is only a few hours away, and we don't want to spoil your appetite."

I was too exhausted to press further.

I wondered if anyone else noticed how Charlie was eyeing Alexa . . .

Chapter 2—The First Meal

After spending more than two months wandering around rocky prairies and weedy foothills by myself (well, me and my shadowy stalker), I felt awkward being offered a soft bed, a clean washroom, and all the utilities I could use. Everything was so neat and organized that it was as if I were renting a room at a motel. Any misgivings I might have held melted like ice as I ran hot water for my shower.

I stepped into the running water and washed off the months of oil and grime from my hair. I then lathered nearly an entire bar of soap on my skin and scrubbed hard enough to almost peel skin. By the time I finished I was red as a boiled lobster, but it was worth it.

When I stepped out of the shower I felt like a civilized man again. Unfortunately, the feeling didn't last long when I saw my reflection in the bathroom mirror. I stopped and stared at myself. My black hair and beard had grown long and scraggly. My unibrow, which I used to try to keep in check, had sprouted and gave the impression a fuzzy caterpillar had taken refuge on my forehead. My hands and feet were calloused, and my skin was leathery and full of scars. But my eyes were the worst. My eyes looked weary and tired. Everything about me was unkempt and overused.

I am a narcissist and a perfectionist, and the man-thing looking at me through the mirror horrified me, but now I had the utilities to fix that and didn't hesitate to begin. I stepped up to the sink, grabbed a pair of scissors and a razor, and began cutting. By the time I was done, I'd cut my beard completely off and shortened my hair to just a few inches. I then moved on to the brow.

After twenty or thirty minutes I examined myself. Without my beard, my face had the slightly gaunt appearance of someone malnourished. I disliked it, but it was much better than before. It also seems I'd acquired a deep tan around my eyes and ears. But on the bright side. my hard life kept me from getting flabby, and my slim body was almost as good as it was in my twenties.

I smiled. "Not perfect, but pretty damn good."

I stepped out of the bathroom a new man. Clean-shaven and groomed, it was as if I'd literally shed an old skin. I felt better than I had in years, but as I looked at the heap of dirty and tattered clothing, I shivered. I'd just showered and I'd rather just wear a towel than climb back into those "well-worn" clothes. Fortunately, before I even touched them, I noticed a note on the bed.

> Dear Mr. Parker,
>
> We assume you would like a change of clothing after refreshing yourself. We selected some clean clothing that might fit you, but feel free to choose something from your closet.
>
> —Management

I smiled. A stocked bathroom *and* new clothes? This place was too much.

As I walked to the closet my shadowy stalker materialized in the corner. "Hey—hey—*hey*! Check you out! You look better than ever! Ha! Where's the other guy I've been following around? But seriously, I wonder what they are going to ask in return for this very friendly treatment."

I scowled.

He sat on a chair off to the side of the room. "I mean, they can't offer this kind of treatment to every drifter who rolls in on their tram."

If I was going to make a good first impression I had to stop talking to imaginary people. It's one thing to have an inner monologue, but speaking to myself out loud was trying the boundaries of sanity. Then again he/it was right. This was pretty good treatment for someone who wandered in out of the dark.

He scratched his head. "They might want something."

I turned away from my specter as he kept talking and began selecting clothes out of the small closet. I found a pair of black cotton slacks, a white T-shirt, a white button-up shirt, a pair of briefs, some black socks, and a pair of strap-on sandals. They all looked out-of-the-box new and were as crisp as a blank piece of paper. I assumed they had been taken from abandoned factories or untouched retail stores.

I put everything on except the sandals. They would have better luck putting those things on a cat. The top shirt was a little too tight around the chest area so I left it unbuttoned over the T-shirt. I caught my reflection in another mirror above a dresser, smiled and posed.

Then everything was cut short when a sudden growl from the inner regions of my stomach reminded me of how hungry I was. The jolly giant Diego told me breakfast is usually served at eight thirty and invited me to join him and my other hosts. He was pretty vague about who else I was going to eat with, so I'd need to be cautious of what I say and do. I smiled.

Being a gracious guest is important, and I would not take this hospitality for granted. Still . . . my first priority was to fill my stomach.

The manifestation spoke up. "I wonder what kind of food they will serve."

I rolled my eyes. "Shut up."

*

When I finished I started to doze, as I hadn't slept well in several days, someone knocked at my door. A booming voice in a Spanish accent rang out. "Parker! It is Diego! I'm here to let you know it's time for—"

I didn't let him finish. I opened the door and with as much patience I could muster, stepped outside and greeted Diego. "Ah, is it time for breakfast? Please, lead the way."

Diego stood and grinned. He was no longer wearing his armor; instead he wore a formal suit and bowtie. It was obvious he was impressed at how much my appearance had changed after shaving and showering. "Mr. Parker! It is good to see you have taken advantage of our facilities."

He clasped my hand in a vigorously friendly handshake and started talking. I didn't hear or understand most of what he was saying because he accidentally slipped in and out of English to Spanish every so often. But I didn't care. All I cared about was the food, so I smiled and nodded as he led me up and down some very impressively furbished stairs and hallways until we reached the entrance to a dining hall. The hall had been decorated to resemble a casual restaurant. There were booths, tables, and a counter with stools; it looked possible to sit at least a couple hundred people. I started to enter, but instead of going into the main hall, Diego continued up another flight of stairs. I hesitated but then followed him up to another dining room.

Diego stopped at a doorway and held the door for me to enter. He smiled broadly. "*Por favour,* enter, enter."

This place had the feel of an upscale restaurant and looked more first class than the other hall. There were plants and a fountain, and the windows were larger and offered a stunning view of the entire compound. Before I could soak up the fantastic view, Diego threw his arm around my shoulders and walked me to a seat at a huge table where about ten men and women sat.

None seemed very impressive to me, but then my eyes were drawn to a man at the head of the table. He sat leaning toward his right with his chin lightly resting on his knuckles. His tanned and defined features emanated a feeling of suave and sophistication. Pushed behind his ears was a mane of long, dark-brown, lightly oiled hair with streaks of gray that reached down to just above the collar of an expensive three-piece suit.

I broke my gaze and looked around the table and stopped on Alexa. She sat near the man with a smile, as if she had remembered a funny joke. She was not in the outfit I saw last night but in clothes that were a little more formal. She wore a pair of tan slacks, a good-looking white blouse, and a woman's jacket. She looked at me and smiled.

I smiled back right before my eardrums ruptured as Diego informed me I was missing something. "Parker! I did not realize, but it looks like you're missing your sandals. Would you like someone you get a pair? We cannot have wandering around in socks."

I smiled slyly. "That won't be necessary. I like strap-ons just about as much as a cat likes water."

Diego laughed his glass-shattering laugh and sat me down in the empty seat at the end of the long table. He stood behind the man at the head of the table. "Parker, your humor is refreshing in this room filled with such serious people. Come, sit here, and let me introduce the members of the council. The person on the left is Mr. Ian Christen, who is our human resources manager. The woman on *his* left is Mrs. Amanda Christen, our treasurer. Together they make sure our people are responsibly managed and adequately compensated. Further up this table is Mrs. Wanda Price, who oversees agriculture and water. The empty seat on Mrs. Price's left belongs to Ms. Heloise Johnson, the head of power management, which I will explain later. This seat here belongs to me. *I* am head of the fort's guard. The man to your immediate right is our construction foreman, Mr. Louis Johansson. He oversees the use of our resources such as construction of buildings and rooms that are needed for our residents. To Johansson's right is Mr. Anthony Turk, who manages miscellaneous businesses such as this restaurant and various records. The empty seat next to Mr. Turk belongs to Mr. Sam, who manages our livestock. To *his* right is someone you already know, Alexa Isabelle Rivera Navarro, and she is our head doctor and part-time teacher for the children. Next to her sits Matthew Navarro, who is our head of fort construction and security, and my grandson-in-law. Finally, this is Alexander Louis Navarro. The man at the head of the table, the current leader of our fort, overseer of all what happens and makes decisions that affect every soul in and on this mountain. He is also my son-in-law."

Diego's chest puffed out as he introduced Navarro, while Navarro looked out the window with minimal interest. Still, I was willing to bet Navarro was aware of everything happening in the room. His eyes shifted toward the door leading to the kitchen. Like me, he seemed ready for the food to be served, and as if on cue, the door opened and a teenager walked in carrying a notepad. She approached each council member to take their breakfast order. When she finally got to me, I could tell she was a little nervous. I didn't look like a savage anymore, but I still have that gaunt, ragged appearance that makes some people cautious.

She swallowed nervously. "What would you like to have for breakfast, sir?"

I smiled. "I'm not sure. What do you have?"

She timidly went down the list. "We have pancakes, waffles, eggs, milk; and fruit. We even have syrup and honey."

I felt excited. "I'll have three waffles with syrup, five scrambled eggs, five of whatever kind of fruit you have, a large slice of ham, and a very tall glass of milk."

She smiled and began to walk away before Alexa interrupted. "I am sorry, but Mr. Parker will have one waffle, two eggs, half an orange, a small slice of ham, and water." Alexa turned toward me. "Mr. Parker, you need to watch what you eat. It's apparent you've eaten very little for quite some time. Your stomach may not be used to eating so much so soon, and if you do not manage what you eat, you may hurt yourself. You may have more food after you have eaten everything on your plate."

I looked at her as if she'd told me I couldn't eat anything at all, and then I realized she was correct. I'd given the same orders to soldiers back in my days as a medic. I nodded and smiled. "I should know better."

She smiled back. While the meals were being prepared, some of the council members asked about what I did before the infection, how far I've traveled, and how long I'd been by myself. Everyone still had more questions but allowed me peace when my food arrived. It might have been more polite to wait for everyone to receive their meals before I started to eat, but after three or four weeks of eating jerky, I couldn't be held responsible for my actions. In fact, I should have received a medal for the way I restrained myself from storming the kitchen and eating everything in sight.

*

I tried not to eat like a ravenous dog, but I still finished my meal before anyone else. I couldn't believe the rest of my hosts were still eating. I decided not to order anything more least my stomach explode (or I vomited), which are both bad first impressions. Hell, I might have pushed my luck when I started eating as if I were in a contest. So I decided to push my dishes away and silently examine my hosts. Many appeared to be around the ages of fifty to sixty, except for Alexa and her husband, Matthew, who both appeared to be in their twenties.

Mr. Navarro was more difficult to read than the others. He cut each bite into a precise size and ate with precise movements while the others ate, but with less focus. Except for Diego, who was much more rowdy. During my short time with him I developed the idea he would prefer to be in a noisy bar playing pool and drinking with other rowdy friends than sitting in a cultured environment. While everyone was quietly taking polite bites, Diego was eating as though he was at a picnic. He shared stories with Alexa and Matthew about things that happened in his past, while they smiled politely and looked at each other with wry expressions.

Ten or fifteen minutes later, just about when people were finishing their meals, an older man with defined wrinkles that extended from his nose past his drooping jowls turned to me.

If I remember correctly, Diego said his name was Ian Christen. "Mr. Parker, I was wondering what your opinion is on the current status of the outside world."

I looked at him. "What do you mean?"

He leaned forward a little. "I'm sorry. What I meant was, how is the world recovering from the event?"

I raised my chin slightly. "You mean the outbreak?"

Ian looked at Amanda and then back to me. "Yes."

I thought for a moment. "I've been traveling around most of Nevada, Mexico, and southern California for . . . I'm actually not sure how long it's been. But during that time, I've found several survivor settlements. Of course none are as successful as yours."

Ian shook his head. "Yes, we are aware of some small outposts, but I am speaking about the status of the infection. How many of those creatures are left?"

I shrugged. "Impossible to tell. Like any infectious disease, this sickness will continue to spread until it burns itself out, but I'm afraid it'll never be completely gone."

Amanda Christen didn't seem satisfied. "What exactly did you do before the infection?"

I smiled politely. "I was a field surgeon for the army."

She said with an air of self-satisfied superiority, "Then tell us what you know about those things."

I narrowed my eyes. "Excuse me?"

She frowned. "You were in the military and have been around them much longer than most of us . . . you *should* know more. How is it they can be shot but not die? Why do they turn into cannibals? Do they starve to death?"

I rested my elbows on the table and thought for a moment. "When I was still in the army, I became friends with a bioengineer. He was a great guy, but he drank too much. One night he got really drunk and told me about a newly discovered bacteria the military was experimenting with. It was supposed to revolutionize soldier performance by enhancing the senses, speed, strength, and endurance."

Alexa interrupted as something dawned on her. "Yes . . . a *bacteria* would explain that odd chemical I've been finding in the *muertos agitados* blood samples I've been collecting."

I looked at Alexa and tilted my head. "Muertos agitados?"

Alexa paused. "The muertos agitados—"the restless dead"—the people who've been infected."

I smiled. "Ah. I just usually heard people call them walkers, stenches, or dead heads."

She smiled back. "Yes. During my free time, I studied the muertos agitados, hoping to learn something useful, such as a way of treating or even curing the infection. Unfortunately, I've haven't been able to prolong the coagulation period long enough to pinpoint the exact cause. At first I thought the source would be found somewhere in or near the brain, since the infection appears to attack the cerebrum, as evident in the disastrous deterioration of the higher brain functions, such as reasoning and memory. Unfortunately, that theory ended when I discovered the deterioration of the cerebrum is just a side effect and not the cause."

I nodded. "I suppose that would explain why their 'sense of self' is replaced with a blinding need to satisfy their supercharged metabolism."

Navarro slightly narrowed his eyes and looked at Alexa. "What else have you learned?"

Alexa looked somewhat nervous under Navarro's full gaze. "When my first theory failed, I tried examining the muertos agitados blood. Unfortunately, the rate of coagulation is too fast, and anything useful fades almost immediately. But if the source is a bacteria like Parker suggests, well, I'll need more time to investigate that possibility."

Mr. Christen raised his hand. "Back to the topic of their mental status. If their existence is driven by their need to eat, why don't they go after each other?"

Alexa stroked her lip, deep in thought. "If it is a bacteria, it is likely it can rewire the body to produce pheromones that say, 'I'm no good to eat.'"

I leaned back in my chair. "Yeah . . . I'm sure they can tell the difference between a walker and a man easily enough with that amazing sense of smell. This is speculation, but I'm sure it's powerful enough that they can detect a man from maybe a mile away, and a wounded man from several more. I'm also pretty sure it's how they are drawn to largely populated areas."

Mrs. Christen frowned. "What about healing? Do those things heal?"

I thought for a second, and then I looked back at my hosts. "Not unless they have a steady supply of food. Otherwise, they won't waste energy regrowing tissue but will just develop enormous scabs."

Almost everyone gagged at that remark, except for Alexa and Navarro. Diego, on the other hand, was drinking some water at the time and shot it out of his nose. Fortunately, he managed to lean away from the table before spraying the ground and bursting into laughter. His son-in-law didn't *seem* too impressed with my story, but the corners of his mouth twitched upward for a second when Diego preformed his spit-take. Alexa was able to keep her composure, but it was apparent that she was a little disappointed with the direction of this conversation.

She looked around. "Perhaps it is time for a change in subject, eh?"

Diego looked at her with an exasperated expression. "Aw, come now, this is the first interesting conversation we have had in months."

She looked at him and rolled her eyes. "Fine. Finish your story, Mr. Parker."

Mrs. Christen interrupted. "Mr. Parker, how can you tell if someone has been infected?"

Before I could say anything, Alexa interjected. "Mrs. Christen, I must have told all of you the five stages at least a dozen times. How can you not know by now?"

It didn't seem as if Alexa was trying to be insulting, but I'm sure Mrs. Christen didn't see it that way. She raised her nose at Alexa. "Oh, I'm sure you've had *plenty* of experience, Mrs. Navarro—"

Alexa cut Ms. Christen off again, but this time she was a little more annoyed. "Contraction, fever, rage, coma, and finally 'death.' Do you think you can hold on to that bit of information?"

It was obvious these two had had some harsh feelings toward one another, but before things escalated further, Navarro interrupted and spoke with an elegant Spanish accent. "It seems Mr. Parker has finished his meal, so perhaps it is time that we allow him to retire to his room so he might rest."

Navarro signaled to a boy standing near the doors. "Cristopher, please escort Mr. Parker back to his room."

The boy hastily nodded. He opened the doors and gestured me to follow him. I nodded toward Navarro and followed the boy out the door and back to my room for some rest.

Chapter 3—Fort Montaña

I sprang up in bed covered in a cold sweat. In the dark I felt a chill run up my spine and heard the deafening beat of my heart in my ears. I'd had one monster of a nightmare.

I shook my head. "I need a shower . . ."

I yanked off my sweaty pajamas and hopped in my private shower when the water became warm enough to take the chill off my skin. I didn't use any soap; it's so hard to come by nowadays that using soap to wash off a light sweat would be a complete waste. Besides, *hot* water is more than relaxing.

But as I stood contently under the running water, my mind drifted back to the fading nightmare. It felt as if I were reliving an old memory, but all my dreams are of me running away from walkers, so I tried not to think about it. I just concentrated on how relaxing this warm shower was.

I eventually got tired of standing and doing nothing so I stepped out of the shower, toweled myself off, I grabbed my toothbrush, and began the monotonous ritual of fighting plaque. About the time I started working on my molars I started considering my options of what I'd do today.

It's been a couple of weeks since I the council decided to grant me citizenship, and offered me a job as an outer-fort messenger or *runner.* Basically the job entailed scouting missions and delivering messages to the forts security outposts in the mountains and dessert. But due to the nature of the occupation (and the fort establishing land-line phones to the outposts) work has become infrequent. So my days are often filled with working out in the private gym, practicing my knife/axe fighting, lending a helping hand to whomever I come across, or just working on various simple projects.

I scratched the prickly hairs on my chin.

Today is a workday, so there won't be many people who'd be free to do much. Maybe a long walk around the fort's wall would help pass the time, or I could find Diego. Sometimes he was fun to be around, if only for brief periods of time.

A shadowy figure appeared in the corner. "Hey, how about we—"

I think I'll take a brisk walk by myself to wake up . . .

He frowned. "Oy! I was speaking. Well, you're thinking I'm speaking—"

A walk by myself before spending some time with Diego . . .

He smiled and shrugged and sat in a chair.

I ignored him and got dressed. Ever since I started living here, I'd been able to ignore the specter more easily. When I put on my new clothing and boots I heaped my sheets onto the floor so the cleaning staff could wash them later and stepped out onto the boardwalk that overlooked a sunny courtyard. I admired the impressive sight of the fort. It had been about five weeks since I'd arrived at La Fort Montaña (which is Spanish for "The Mountain Fort") and I still hadn't gotten used to the sights. According to Diego, the fort first belonged to his grandfather, who built it out of fear of the world ending in 2012. Looking around, I can see he had an interesting vision of what his shelter should be like.

The fort lies on the floor of a dried canyon that winds through tall and nearly impassible mountains. The fort is five miles from the canyon's entrance, less than half a mile wide, and is approximately twelve miles long. Behind the fort is a modest dam that supplies the fort's water and a small amount of its power. I'm not sure what they do about drainage or sewage.

Along each wall were multistory buildings carved and paved into the canyon. In total there were four or five dozen buildings devoted to businesses and several hundred for living quarters. Yet there was always new construction to meet the demand for the expanding population.

However, stone and cement buildings were not the only things being constantly added. Diego and his family spend years commissioning artisans to "beautify" Fort Montaña. His theory was, "Beauty will raise the spirits of people above the fear of the outside world," and he might be right; people were happy here. So they spent time and resources cultivating trees and bushes and erecting statues and fountains for parks in the center of the canyon for the public to enjoy.

But in my opinion, the most impressive part of this fort was the carved slopes of the mountains. Massive terraces filled with crops of fruits, grains, and vegetables had been carved into the fertile soil of the surrounding mountains. There was a variety of domesticated animals on a several-mile-long pasture above the canyon. The fort kept sheep, chickens, bees, horses, and cattle. All were used for food products and services they could provide, like meat, milk, cheese, eggs, soap, wool, honey, wax, pollination, heavy labor, and leather. The beautiful surroundings, the order, the safety—these things let the troubled soul breathe easily.

Well, almost . . .

Like the living dead, Charlie skulked my way. Every time I crossed paths with the little bastard, he ended up giving me the stink-eye followed by threats and was usually stopped by a passing guard or Diego. Still, I didn't want to spend this beautiful day staring daggers at the little punk, I wanted a relaxing walk, so I gave him a wide berth and continued on my way.

Unfortunately, he wasn't as courteous. He locked on to me and gave me the stink-eye until I passed, and then he turned and started to follow me.

I turned to face him. "What do you want?"

He smiled grimly. "Well, well, well, the big man finally decides to dig his head out of his *ass* to talk to me."

I didn't blink. "What do you want?"

He threw his arms up. "Riddle me this, Pops! How is it you have been here for five weeks and have one of the best jobs in this hellhole while I have been here my entire life and don't have shit?"

By now he was inches from me, and I could smell him. Charlie had the hygiene routine of a month-old corpse, and every time I got close to him, I felt as if I needed a shower.

He smiled smugly. "What is it, *old man*? Did I hurt your feelings?"

I smiled back. "Hey, Charlie . . . how's Alexa been doing?"

He looked confused. "What?"

I caught him off guard. "Well, I know you've been stalking her. Jealously watching her from behind the bushes with your pants down—"

His eyes filled with white-hot anger. "*You fu—*"

I didn't let him finish. As he moved to throw a punch, I hurled a strong uppercut against the bottom of his jawbone. For a split second all of his weight was gone, just before collapsing in a heap on the ground. I looked at the crumpled mess at my feet and massaged my knuckles. He looked like an unwashed jacket on the floor of some teenager's bedroom. This wasn't the first time he tried to harass me, but this *was* the first time I knocked him out. I wondered about the repercussions of what I'd done. Charlie was the nephew of council members Ian and Amanda Christen, and it was well known they were extremely protective of him. It was because of their influence that he became a guard instead of shoveling garbage or cleaning sewage. Still, the most infuriating thing was how his aunt and uncle turned a blind eye and a deaf ear to all the "circumstantial" harassment complaints, yet they saw and heard clearly enough when people pushed back and he got hurt. And I *did* hurt him. He might have needed a trip to the dentist. A pit formed in my stomach. I may be higher up on the food chain than he was, but I wasn't untouchable.

I closed my eyes and took a deep breath. I learned from my army days that your worst enemy in a battlefield situation is your imagination. So I took a moment to predict the most plausible outcome. The Christens would definitely react aggressively. They might go as far as trying to get me expelled from the fort on a "use of excessive force" charge. If they tried anything, I'd just turn this back on Charlie and finally get this schizophrenic freak booted to a position with less power. In any case I was not going to spend today worrying about a couple of crooked politicians and their brat. I'd burn that bridge when I got to it.

My shadow appeared behind me. "Funny that you call this kid schizophrenic."

I froze and let out an annoyed sigh. My phantom jumped out from behind the bushes with a crooked smile that curved along his face.

I glare at him. "I thought I ditched you."

He knelt and looked at Charlie. "I'll always be around whenever you're worried about something."

I folded my arms. "I'm not worried."

He looked at me with a smile. "You can't lie to yourself."

I shook my head. "Shut up."

He stood up. "So . . . we're just going to leave him here?"

There was no way this guy was going to disappear, unless—

Diego walked around a corner and spied me. "Ah! *Parker!* It's good to see you!"

I smiled as my phantom vanished and Diego approached in his long, confident stride. "Hello, Diego. I can see that today is especially entertaining to you."

Diego looked past me, saw Charlie on the ground, and let out a tired sigh, his good mood fading like an old tattoo. "I see Charlie got on your bad side."

I smiled. "Like hell he did. The little parasite tried to attack me."

Diego cocked an eyebrow. "Really? I knew he was increasingly violent, but attacking someone? What did you do?"

I put on an innocent face. "I was enjoying a quiet and beautiful morning."

Diego looked at Charlie. "I suppose I will have to put him on suspension . . . again. That boy has never been anything but trouble, but for the last few wee—" Diego made an Ah-ha! expression as a thought popped into his mind. "Parker! He must be jealous of you!"

I rolled my eyes as he continued.

"Yes! I think it was around the time I gave you your job that he started becoming more and more aggressive. His little outbursts have always been a nuisance, but they got worse when you came along."

Diego marveled at his idea and signaled a few men to come over and take Charlie to the infirmary. Once they were out of sight, we turned and started a relaxed walk up a stairway that led to a private sentry walk that extended the length of the fort and ended at the main gate.

Diego put a hand on my shoulder. "Don't worry, my friend, I don't blame you for Charlie's jealousy. Now, what are we going to do—"

I raised my hand. "Diego, when did Matt and Alexa get married?"

Diego raised his eyebrows. "Now what does that have to do with anything?"

I smiled. "Just humor me."

Diego thought for a moment. "Hmmm . . . about three weeks ago, but I don't see how—"

I nodded. "That's around the same time you gave me my job."

Diego looked at me quizzically.

I rolled my eyes. "Charlie isn't jealous of me, he's jealous of Matt."

Diego looked at me for a second, still trying to register what I had said. "What?"

I tried again. "Haven't you noticed Charlie's obsession with Alexa? He wasn't getting more aggressive because of me but because Matthew and Alexa got married. His temper escalating and my getting my job are purely coincidental."

Diego was starting to put the pieces together and was getting angry for not realizing it sooner. "Then all those outbursts—"

I furrowed my brow. "Diego, haven't you noticed Charlie stalking Alexa?"

Diego's face turned red. *"¡Y no va a salirse con la suya—!"*

I stopped Diego pre-rant. "Diego! Do not lose your composure. At the next assembly I'll request that Charlie be removed from the guard on the grounds of irresponsible and blatant abuse of power. I believe it would be better for you to be a witness and supporter of my idea than the plaintiff."

Diego began to calm down. "Sí—yes . . . I suppose so. You speak with sensible words, my friend. Very well, I will go along with your plan, Parker."

Chapter 4—Sam the Rancher

Diego and I walked around discussing our plan of action on the three-mile walk to the fort's gate. Actually, he only ranted about what he would do to Charlie if he hurt Alexa or her beloved husband, Matthew, how he was so proud of them, and how we were going to demote Charlie to garbage collector after the hearing. By the time all the air was out of Diego's sails it was noon, and we were at the sentry walk on the wall. It was around then he realized he missed breakfast because of his little tirade and was feeling hungry. So I suggested he go meet with some of his men for lunch. As I watched and he descended the stairway into an open-air restaurant, I couldn't help but feel relieved he left. Spending time with Diego was exhausting and can be even worse when he was venting his anger. I was worn out.

I looked around and admired the view. I could see everything from the sentry walk. Behind the fort wall was a large park surrounded by popular restaurants that served foods grown independently from the main fields, and stores that sold handmade clothing, toys, or basic tools retrieved from ghost towns. There was even a stage where artisans could display their wares, where singers could sing, and where musicians could play music when not at their day job. Whenever people weren't working, they came down to this amazing courtyard to relax and enjoy some of the comforts that had been lost during the outbreak. I'd become accustomed to life beyond these walls, and sometimes I kind of missed the danger and the open spaces . . .

I thought I'd go for a walk through the canyon. A couple of days ago Diego mentioned something about the head rancher, Sam, moving to the canyon entrance to take advantage of more space for his animals, and I thought it might be a good idea to get to know him.

*

For several hours I walked along the cool canyon floor and enjoyed the silence of a summer afternoon. Everything seemed at peace—not the same kind of peace behind the fort walls, but rather a quiet peace . . . except the canyon was hardly a safe place to be. At the mouth of the canyon were eight tiers cut into the walls, each sporting high-powered armaments. I hadn't noticed them when I first arrived, but apparently several tiers hold things called Hotchkiss revolving cannons. And beside each cannon sat several miniguns with an imposing amount of ammunition. I'm sure it would take an impressive force to get through the mouth of the canyon.

Still, the mouth wasn't the most dangerous part. A little while before I arrived a scientist managed to trade residence for himself and his surviving family for the secret to making something called Greek fire. Apparently, he rediscovered some kind of flammable liquid that grows when someone attempts to douse it with water. Navarro was very impressed and ordered the mass production of the stuff, and later, Matthew came up with an idea to install reservoirs inside the canyon walls to dispense the Greek fire and redirect some water pipes to accelerate the fire's growth. So anything that got past the guns at the mouth of the canyon would get burned by an unquenchable fire.

A shiver ran up my spine and I mused about the elegance of this death trap . . . that is, until I heard the rumbling. The ground started to tremble as something big charged around the bend.

My stalker looked around. "We should probably go back."

I nodded. "Shut up . . . and you might have a point—"

In an instant, a massive, hairy wall rounded the bend and stampeded in my direction.

Both my stalker and I jumped out of our skins.

"Holy—"

"Crap!"

I looked around, hoping to see something I could use to get out the way. The distance of the charging wall closed in on me fast.

The shadow man jumped back. "*Crap!* Crap, crap, crapcrapcrapcrapcrap, *crap!*"

I frantically looked around. "Shut up!"

I ran to a depression in the canyon wall and flatted myself against it. In seconds, nearly a hundred cattle flew past. After several beats, ten men on horseback bolted past in a full gallop, each whoopin' and hollerin' as they chased the herd. When I realized I was safe I let my head drop. My heart pounded in my ears as I panted. What the hell was that about?

As my heart rate slowed, a guy on a horse trotted up to me. He wore a ten-gallon hat and was dressed in denim. "Hey there! Y'all okay?"

I looked at him as if he was insane.

He leaned forward onto the horn of his light tan saddle. "Y'all look like long-tailed cat in a room full o' rockin' chairs."

I stared at him with an exasperated expression and asked, "You wouldn't happen to be looking for ten cowboys and a big herd of cattle?"

He slapped his leg and laughed. "Ha! Not really, but ah have been following one for about three miles."

I nodded, still glued to the wall. "Is there a reason they're rampaging through the canyon?"

The man eyed me through a pair of squinty eyes firmly set behind a deeply suntanned and leathery face. "Exercise, pard'ner, but ah can think of a better question. What are you doin' down here?"

I peeled myself from the wall. "Exercise, pard'ner. You wouldn't happen to be the rancher Diego's been talkin' about?"

He grinned. "Well ah'm a rancher, and ah do know Diego. Name's Sam."

I walked up to him and extended my hand. "It's a pleasure; my name's Parker."

Sam shook my hand and cocked an eyebrow. "You're Parker? Damn, it sure is a treat meeting you. Hell, y'all's the reason the upper crust is letting me keep my herd in the fields. Hey, how 'bout y'all come onto the ranch and we can share a couple of drinks? But right now y'all best hide behind that rock 'cause the herd's comin' back."

Sure enough the earth started trembling as a hairy wall stampeded my way again. I decided to take Sam's advice and crouched behind a rock.

*

A few hours later I was at the Halfway Ranch, leaning on a fence post drinking cool water with the head rancher, Sam.

Together we watched the ranch hands ride off into the distance to a nearby valley where the cattle would be left to graze before being called back before nightfall. At sunset the ranch hands would turn the herd around and bring them back.

When they disappeared over the horizon, I took a drink of water and looked up at the revolving cannons embedded in the canyon's mouth.

Sam took a sip and looked at me. "So, were you really wanderin' 'round for ten years by yerself?"

I paused before taking a sip from my drink. "Hmmm?"

Sam nodded and leaned against the fence. "See, ah hear before y'all moseyed in like a stray cat, y'all wandered around the entire country by yourself. Goin' 'round an' fightin' with your bare hands every ahgitado muerto and psycho that crossed your path."

I lowered my drink and raised my eyebrows. "Hmmm . . . well, I did fight a lot of highwaymen, but I usually just picked up and snuck away from walkers."

Sam turned and looked into the distance. "Walkers? Huh . . . ah like that . . . easier ta say than ahgitado muertos. Anyway, so all them stories floatin' 'round aren't true?"

I held up my hand as I swallowed a mouthful of water. "Well, some are. I've been alone for quite some time, and I've sometimes had to fight to get by."

Sam turned back to me. "Ah heard you once fought and killed 'bout fifty of the Hord's gang members for terrorizing a small town."

I smiled. "Nah . . . the gang only had like twenty members, and the only reason I did anything was because the sheriff hired me."

Sam raised his eyebrows. "How'd that happen?"

I sighed and scratched my head. "At the time I was wandering through a prairie in New Mexico and had just about run out of food and water. But right before I died of dehydration, I stumbling upon a small town called Perfection. Actually, Perfection wasn't so much of a town as much as it was a jumble of houses and a hundred or so survivors."

Sam nodded.

I ran my fingers through my hair. "Anyway, the people weren't too excited to see a stranger walk in from out of the blue asking for food and water. They were even less thrilled when he had nothing to trade. It wasn't long after that they started suggesting I move on. When I was just about to collapse from exhaustion, the sheriff took me back to his station and gave me some water and a meal."

Sam smiled. "Sounds like mah kind of guy."

I grinned. "Yeah, it was the best meal I ever had. Afterward we started talking, but before we could really get into a conversation, he heard an air-raid siren and ran to a back room."

Sam nodded again. "All right . . ."

I let out a deep breath. "That's when hell started breaking loose. The siren was an alarm to signal the town was under attack from the Hord. Most rode on noisy choppers up and down streets chasing the townspeople back into their homes while some raided barns and stores for supplies."

Sam leaned against the fence with a grimace. "Lowdown cowards."

I half-smiled. "Yeah, except there wasn't much in the way of destruction. Their attack looked showier than anything else. If they wanted real damage, they would have smashed windows and started fires . . . it seemed they were only making a lot of noise."

Sam looked a little puzzled. "What did you do?"

I turned back to the empty fields. "After raiding for general supplies, one of 'em broke into a house and started dragging out a woman. I tried to stop him but I was still too weak to do anything but bluff and brandish my weapons. Thankfully the sheriff stepped out and blew the guy away with a pump-action shotgun."

Sam clapped his hands. "Good on 'im."

I shook my head. "It seemed like a great idea at the time, but no . . . it was a bad move. After the sheriff killed one, they turned more aggressive. After the woman ran back into her house, the guys on the choppers surrounded us and began to fire. They could have stormed the station but they had to leave."

Sam turned to me and raised his eyebrows. "Why?"

I half-smiled. "The trucks were driving away and so were the escorts. Still, that didn't stop one of 'em from leaving behind a live grenade to blow up one of the sheriff's front porch. Anyway, after they were gone the sheriff called an emergency town meeting. He wanted to form a posse and pursue the raiders onto the prairie. He tried appealing to the people's anger and desire to be rid of the constant threat, but no one shared his boldness. Things were only made worse when the mayor took the stage. With his smooth tongue he promised the bikers wouldn't return anytime soon, that fighting them would only provoke a worse attack, and convinced everyone they would lose against the bikers."

Sam looked annoyed. "Sounds like a coward."

I nodded. "He was. He was a terrible mayor and was losing favor to the sheriff before the bikers arrived. It was only after they started attacking the town that he started regaining popularity."

Sam looked at me. "Why?"

"The only way he knew how to hold on to power was by playing on people's fear. Eventually the people fell for his empty promises. Still, the sheriff wouldn't give up on his people even though they turned their backs on the sheriff's ideas."

Sam started to calm down but still looked annoyed. "What happened after that?"

I stared into the distance. "The sheriff gathered all the ammunition he could carry and started to march on the Hord."

Sam snorted. "Not too smart, but at least the man had nerve."

I shook my head. "The man had a death wish. Good thing I stopped him by offering a smarter plan."

Sam grinned. "What did y'all do?"

I gulped the last of my water. "If he would give me three weeks I would infiltrate the gang and weaken the resolve and trust among the leader and his men. Then I would spread rumors about how the entire town had rallied behind the sheriff and were arming themselves and planning an attack."

Sam stared at me with awe. "How the *hell* did you manage to pull off a stunt like that?"

"I didn't. When I tracked the bikers back to their base, I discovered the infamous Hord were mainly guys trying to feed their families."

Sam was confused. "What?"

I nodded. "Yeah . . . the so-called Hord were actually a small community living out of caves feeding off small animals and whatever they could steal from surrounding settlements. They hyped up their own status by spreading rumors about how dangerous they were so no one would try a counterattack."

Sam rubbed his eyes. "So if y'all didn't compromise the gang, what did y'all do?"

I started toying with my cup. "I talked. I infiltrated their ranks like I originally planned, but instead of spreading rumors I pieced together both sides of the story. It turned out the members belonged to a town that came under attack from a roaming herd of walkers. After their homes were destroyed they had to resort to violent tactics. In the end I found out they weren't really that bad."

Sam looked confused. "Then why did that guy try to kidnap that girl?"

"I later learned she belonged to their community but was separated when the town was destroyed. The only reason she thought she was being kidnapped was the gang had masks on and she didn't recognize them. Anyway, they were led by a pretty nasty character named Smith. He was the reason they didn't try to settle. He figured the people were more easily controlled if they had to rely on him to survive."

Sam shook his head. "Soun's like a damn snake."

I put my cup down on a fence post and cracked my knuckles. "Well, that isn't the worst part. It turned out Smith struck a deal with Perfection's mayor. Whenever the mayor started to lose favor, he would call the Hord to put the fear back into the people."

Sam hit the fence with a gloved palm and stood up fuming. "Let me guess, he told lies so well a man would be a fool not to believe them."

I nodded again. "Yeah, I know. In any case, I had to relay this information. At the first chance I got I went back to Perfection and told the sheriff. He wanted to kill the mayor, but I convinced him otherwise. Instead, he started tailing the mayor while I worked on Smith from the other end. Eventually we found out where they usually met. When they were together, we used an old camcorder the sheriff had stashed away and taped their meeting. After that it wasn't too much trouble to out the two and establish a cease-fire between Perfection and the 'Hord.' After a little doing, I managed to convince Perfection to adopt the Hord and their families."

Sam laughed. "How did you do *that*?"

I smiled. "I convinced the town that if they couldn't fight off a bunch of guys on dirt bikes and choppers, they needed people who could. So I nominated the Hord."

Sam looked puzzled. "Wouldn't those guys just raise more hell?"

I smiled again. "Who knows? I didn't stick around much longer afterward."

Sam frowned. "Why not?"

I laughed. "The sheriff found out I got too friendly with his daughter."

Sam and I had a nice hard laugh.

Sam tried to catch his breath. "Damn, Parker, y'all sure know how to fix and screw things up."

I wiped a tear from my eye. "I do my best . . . by the by, what do you do with the animals if a walker shows up?"

Sam grinned. "Depends."

I could tell he was waiting for me to say, "Depends on what?"

Sam leaned against his fence. "My men an' ah can handle just 'bout anythin' that wanders our way, but just in case, I train 'em to let the animals loose and drive 'em north."

I cocked an eyebrow. "What's up north?"

Sam gestured loosely up the mountain range. "A couple miles down yonder is a long trail that leads up in the mountains. We drive 'em up there whenever the weather takes a turn for the worse, someone tries to attack us, or a group of walkers we can't handle show up."

I thumbed toward the canyon. "Why not put them there?"

Sam rolled his eyes. "'Cause that's a dead end. Ya never put anything worth savin' in a dead end."

I took a moment to think about his debatable opinion before shrugging and looking down at my empty tin cup. "If you say so, Sam."

Sam grinned and raised his eyebrows. "What about walkers? What was the biggest one you ever took down?"

I thought. "Hmmm . . . let's see . . . a while back I came across an old ghost town where I thought I could replenish my supplies and maybe stay a night or two. But as soon as I investigated a rundown corner store, a six foot, four-hundred-pound walker charged me. He was fresh, so he was fast, but he wasn't any good at grabbing faster opponents. So as he charged me I tripped him up and put him down by slamming my axe into the back of his neck."

Sam smiled. "Aw, I got one that's better than that. A few years back I was doing a scouting mission deep in the mountains when I saw this group of walkers chasing after a small herd of deer."

I cocked an eyebrow. "And? There's nothing strange about that—"

Sam smiled. "No, there isn't . . . except one of them was Christina Turk."

I thought for a moment. "Turk . . . the actress?"

Sam's smile broadened. "Yup."

I shook my head. "Huh . . . what a waste."

Sam nodded. "I know, she was a beaut."

Sam and I spent a few more hours telling big fish stories about our various encounters with walkers. I told a story about how I had to fight ten fresh walkers to get out of a mega-store, and he told one about how he put down an infected mountain lion. But we had to wrap things up when the evening round-up approached and he had to take off.

Chapter 5—Blue Eyes Blue

I lay under my favorite apple tree in a depression. A few days after my encounter with Charlie, and with much protest from his aunt and uncle, Navarro authorized a court-martial to question Charlie's ability to perform his duties. While that was a small victory, I hadn't made any progress since. I'd visited the security and record stations several times to find grievance and incident reports concerning Charlie, but didn't find *anything* useful.

I hated to admit it, but the Christens were a step ahead of me. Only people with their clearance had the access and power to doctor or erase reports. And I supposed if anyone tried submitting follow-up reports, they would somehow be silenced. The Christens were pretty good at intimidating Charlie's victims. I wondered if the victims would even talk if I approached them.

"What you need are victims who have already lost everything or are too stupid to be afraid of the Christen family."

I turned away from my least-favorite stalker. "Huh . . . is asking you to go away out of the question?"

The phantom chuckled. "You're catchin' on. I'm going nowhere."

I got up. I briefly looked at the dark figure sitting on the ground and grinning under *my* tree. "Whatever . . ."

He watched me with the same smug expression a cat gives a person who claims to own it. "You know I'm right. There is no one more dangerous than someone whose only possession is a grudge. Find people whose lives have been made completely miserable by the Christens."

I reached upward and examined an apple that didn't seem ready to be picked quite yet. "Let's see . . . Charlie is a part of the police force . . . so he practically has access to every inch of the fort that's open to the general public. He also has a huge inferiority complex that often leads him to abuse his power by going after women, children, and animals. However, he has the protection of his aunt and uncle. He'll pick fights with men he knows are cowards or are smart enough not to fight back."

The man in black chuckled again. "You've listed a broad spectrum of people. What are you going to do with that information?"

I thought a moment and spoke without really thinking. "I think I'll start with women who have recently been widowed. I'm sure Charlie has tried to take advantage of their mental distress, and I'm sure they'd love an outlet to release their anger."

The man in black smiled mischievously. "Now *that* sounds like a plan I can get behind."

I closed my eyes. There was nothing worse than being sincerely complimented by him . . . we'd find Alexa and start after lunch.

*

Being the head physician for the fort, Alexa had access to all documents concerning accident-related deaths and injuries. My—*his* idea—was finding people who've been "assaulted", but common traits among women are often reluctant to give details on *who* assaulted them. If I could find anything useful,

I could ask the victims for more information and maybe fill out official reports that wouldn't disappear.

Unfortunately, Alexa shot down that idea by claiming doctor-patient confidentiality. "I'm sorry, Mr. Parker, but I can't divulge that information without the willing consent of my patients."

She was playing hardball, so I decided to take a more direct approach.

On a Saturday afternoon I briefly walked through clinics, cafes, and restaurants, proclaiming to the masses that Charlie Christen was going to face a court-martial and I was heading the case. "If anyone wants that dirty cop canned, then come to me and give a story and report. I promise you'll never be bullied by him and his, ahem, accomplices again! Spread the word to meet me at the Sweet Grill on Monday if you are brave enough to come forward!"

After an entire weekend of making a fool of myself, the fort was buzzing about Charlie's hearing. But the best part was when Charlie's aunt showed up outside my apartment. "How *dare* you spread that *confidentia—don't you close that doo—I'll have Navarro expel you! I swear it!*"

I especially loved it when she started pounding open-handed on my door when I closed it in her face. Unfortunately my open-air tactic didn't work as well as I had hoped. Monday morning arrived and no one showed up. It was possible people weren't stepping forward because they feared the court-martial would be dropped and they'd suffer blowback for their participation.

"Ya wan' anythin' else, Mr. Parker?"

I politely shook my head as the waitress poured. "Coffee's fine, ma'am."

She gave me a grim look and nodded. "Ya know, it's the strangest thang. This place is usually so busy this time o' day."

I shrugged and gave her a sincere smile.

"Looks like things aren't going your way, slugger . . ."

I rolled my eyes as the waitress walked away and the man in black slid into my booth. "Are you really going to do this now?"

He grinned. "You know, I'm beginning to think the Christens have covered all their bases."

I looked away from his smug expression. "I have no idea what to do next. There are no incident reports. I can't get access to the damn medical records, and I've practically dragged my reputation through the mud while at the same time losing all confidence among the freakin' *sheeple* in the fort."

The man in black smiled and disappeared as a timid voice approached me from behind. "Um . . . Mr. Parker?"

I arched my neck as a scrawny girl who looked to be eight and in a pair of overalls walked slowly toward me. "Yes?"

She looked down with a sad expression. Her dirty blonde hair fell and covered her face. "Um . . . my name is Tiffany . . . an' I want to . . ."

I watched her twist her foot on the ground and shove her hands deep into her Levi's pockets. "I'm here to . . . to . . ."

I finished her sentence. "To talk about Charlie?"

She nodded.

I gestured across from me. "Have a seat, Tiffany."

She walked over and awkwardly climbed up. In the sunlight I could see a light coat of freckles on her flushed cheeks. The waitress walked over when she noticed my new guest and offered a glass of juice.

Tiffany shook her head. "No thank you, ma'am."

"Are you sure, hon?"

Tiffany nodded. "Thank you, ma'am."

As the waitress smiled and walked away to attend to some other tedious task, I turned back to Tiffany and set down a tape recorder on the table. "Do you mind if I record this?"

She shook her head.

"Now, what is your full name?"

She looked at the tape recorder. "Tiffany Addams."

I smiled. "And what about Charlie?"

Tiffany put on a serious expression. "He killed my mom an' dad."

I was taken completely off guard. "What?"

She nodded furiously. "My dad beat him up for doing something bad to my mom, an' the next day a mean old woman came an' yelled at him, but then my dad called her a dumb punt or somethin'. Then men came to our home and started breakin' things. When my dad tried to stop them they broke his arm. After that my mom started cryin' 'cause we lost our wages . . ."

I sat silently, completely engrossed in her story as Tiffany started to lose her self-control. "An' . . . an' when my . . . my mom and dad w-went to work . . . they . . . they . . . didn' . . . didn'."

Her sad blue eyes teared up before she burst out sobbing. She was unable to bring herself to say they died. I looked around and saw the waitresses and the cooks standing behind the counter listening to Tiffany's story with watering eyes. Before anyone could say anything, an old woman walked in the door and looked around. When she spotted Tiffany, she frowned and started toward us. I grabbed the recorder and shoved it in the pocket of my jacket without turning it off.

She came at us with long and frustrated strides. "*Tiffany Addams*! You know better than to run off like that!"

I tried to look as innocent as possible when she Tiffany's eyes were red and puffy. She turned to me and frowned at me accusingly. "Who are you?"

I thought carefully about what I was going to say next. "No one of consequence. Are you Tiffany's mother?"

She folded her arms. "I'm her caseworker. Tiffany's mother is—"

I raised my eyebrows as she caught herself from saying Tiffany's mother was dead, but that didn't stop Tiffany from tearing up again.

"Are you going to take her to her father then?" I asked.

Tiffany and the restaurant staff looked a little confused.

The social worker glowered at me and spoke in an angry, hushed tone. "She doesn't have one."

I looked at Tiffany and then back to the woman. "Then may I ask who you are?"

She huffed. "Ms. Quadson."

I turned to Tiffany and smiled. "Thank you, Tiffany, you've been very helpful."

Over the next several days Tiffany's story weaved throughout the fort as the restaurant staff spread it. And it wasn't long until dozens of people came to me to submit their stories and provide their official statements.

A few days later I decided to swing by the . . . I don't think we have an orphanage . . . I had to think really hard about where I had to go to find children who'd lost their parents. Normally I'd go to the head of human resources to find out where to find orphaned kids, except the head was Mr. Christen, and we aren't on speaking terms right now.

Alexa was the doctor and a part-time teacher. She'd know.

*

"Mr. Parker, why do you want to know?" Alexa gave me a stern look.

I tried to be as charming as possible. "It was the little girl, Tiffany, who started the ball rolling when I was gathering the statements I want to use as evidence. I want to thank her."

Alexa crossed her arms and looked out the window. "I don't feel comfortable with children being exploited, even if there's a good reason. Some people say the end justifies the means, but I don't always believe that."

I ran my fingers through my hair. "Alexa . . ."

She looked at me with eyes without compromise. "I will tell you where she is *if* you swear you will not use her testimony at the hearing."

I didn't know what to say . . . Tiffany's speech was the most tear-jerking piece of evidence I had. Her statement could cinch the entire case even if I had to give up half the statements I'd collected. But Alexa was uncompromising in her beliefs. It was probably because she feared I'd try to recruit Tiffany as a witness . . . which was a bad thing.

I sighed. "I'm sorry, Alexa, but I can't do that."

Alexa looked disappointed. "Then I will not help you."

*

I felt terrible . . . but Alexa had a point. Using Tiffany any more would be wrong. I needed a drink, but unfortunately, the fort did not have the capability of producing its own alcohol, or at least anything decent, so I settled for a cold glass of apple juice from the Sweet Grill.

Ever since I'd used the Grill as my base of operations, they'd seen an upswing in business. As people waited in line to give their statements, they bought and developed a taste for the Grill's apple pie (which I was already fond of) and became repeat patrons. The owners were so thankful, they decided to give me a free drink and slice of pie every time I visit their restaurant. I decided to avoid the apple pie, least I lose my slim figure.

I sat at my usual booth.

Mrs. Perchuhi walked over with her notepad ready. She didn't care for me at first, but since I managed to increase business we've become well acquainted. "Parker?"

I sat my slightly worn hat on the tabletop. "Just juice today."

She nodded. "Ya sure ya don't wan' anythin' else?"

I politely shook my head as she left to get my drink. Alexa had made me feel like a real jackass, and I—

"Is Mr. Parker here today?"

I looked over my shoulder and saw one of the waitresses looking over the countertop at a kid. "He's right over there—"

The kid glanced my way and then ran in my direction when she spotted me. I was pleasantly surprised when I realized it was Tiffany.

She spoke so fast I could barely understand what she was trying to say. *"MrParkerMrParkerShe's—"*

With a little squeak Tiffany slipped under my table and out of sight as the door flew open. "Where is she?"

I again looked over my shoulder and saw Ms. Quadson speaking harshly to Mrs. Perchuhi. Perchuhi never took kind to people yelling in her restaurant. "Where's *who?"*

Quadson was fuming. *"The little girl!"*

The room quieted down. Perchuni shook her head and waved across the room to demonstrate the variety of little children eating with their parents. She covertly glanced at me long enough to see me lightly shake my head.

Mrs. Perchuni looked back at Quadson with her tongue against her cheek. *"Well?* There are quite a few little girls here, you see one you like?"

Quadson looked around briefly before storming out. Not only was she mad she didn't find Tiffany, she was embarrassed she had made a scene.

After she left, the cold silence began to thaw and the patrons started talking again. Many of the conversations started off with, "What was that about?"

Perchuni walked over with my glass of apple juice. "Parker, why's it seem every week you come in, someone else comes in angry?"

I smiled. "Must be my charming personality."

She put her hands on her hips. "It was bad enough Charlie came in lookin' for you and the Christens came in tryin' to shut us down 'cause of you, but now we have her too? I'm startin' to think you are more trouble than you're worth."

I shrugged. "I'm sorry to put you in this situation, but I promise it'll all end after the trial."

Perchuni push her tongue against her cheek. "It better." She might have been annoyed with me, but her mood lightened when she noticed Tiffany peering around the side of my seat. "Oh, hon', are you okay?"

Tiffany quietly looked up and nodded. "Yes'm."

Perchuni smiled and carefully crouched down to her level. "How 'bout you come out of there?"

Tiffany nodded and crawled out. When she stood up, Mrs. P. lightly dusted her shoulders and sat her down in my booth. "How 'bout a slice o' pie . . . on the house."

Tiffany glanced at me and then back at Perchuni. "No, thank you."

She smiled. "If you change your mind, just let me know. M'kay?"

Tiffany nodded.

Mrs. P. gave me a stern glance and then walked away.

Ever since Tiffany told her stirring story at the restaurant, she'd been the favorite of the cooks and waitresses. Even though Quadson forbade her from coming back ever since she started the ball rolling on my project.

She didn't appear well. Her face was ashen, her hair tangled, and it looked as if she'd been crying. Her clothing was wrinkled and dusty, as if someone hadn't washed them properly.

"Mr. Parker, I need to ask you a favor."

I took a sip of my apple juice. "Depends . . . I don't do assassinations—"

Mrs. P. slapped the back of my head. She'd come back to give Tiffany a small plate of scrambled eggs, sausage, and buttered toast. "Stop with the jokes and listen." Mrs. P. softened and placed a fork and the plate on the table. "Here ya go, hon. You didn't ask for 'em, but I know a hungry child when I see one."

Mrs. P. and I heard Tiffany's stomach growl when she stared at the plate. We smiled as she glanced at us and started eating as if someone was going to take it away. Mrs. P. smiled at me, and then she slapped the back of my head again. "Don't you dare tease this poor girl again."

I rubbed the back of my head and smiled. "No, ma'am."

Mrs. P. looked sternly at me, smiled at Tiffany, and then walked away.

Tiffany was already halfway through her meal, so I decided to watch the crowd outside until she finished.

*

When she finished, she quietly cleared her throat to get my attention. I looked back at Tiffany. "Finished?"

She nodded.

I leaned forward and rested my elbows on the table. "You wanted to ask for a favor?"

She nodded quickly.

I sighed and smiled. "Ask away."

She looked down. "Well . . . since I helped you . . . you need to help me, right?"

I cocked an eyebrow. "That's usually how favors work."

She tried to avoid eye contact. "I wanted to ask you to . . ."

I raised my eyebrows. "Something tells me this is going to be a big favor."

She unconsciously raised her sleeve to rub her upper arm. "Um . . ."

I saw bruise marks . . . the kind that look like someone grabbed her roughly. I looked away. "You know . . ."

She looked up.

I gave my most comforting smile. "Whenever someone needs to say something embarrassing, it's best they say it really fast."

She nodded.

I cocked an eyebrow. "On the count of three, just say it . . . one—"

"Ineedyoutoadoptmeandmysisters!"

I paused and tried to make sense of what she'd said. "That sounded like—"

She exhaled and spoke in a more even tone. "I need you to adopt me and my sisters."

I blinked, still not sure what to say. "Adopt? Sisters?"

Tiffany drew in a deep breath, as if she were about to plunge into a cold pond. "Mrs. Quadson took me and my little sister in when our parents . . ." She swallowed back the tears and looked at me with conviction. "When our parents died."

I interlaced my fingers and rested my chin on them.

She continued. "She was okay at first . . . but after I went to talk to you, she started being mean. Especially after I spied on her talking with Mrs . . . . um . . . Chris . . . um . . ."

A pit formed in my stomach. "Ms. Amanda Christen?"

She nodded. "Yeah, that's her. Mrs. Christen was angry with Mrs. Quadson for letting me see you. Mrs. Quadson said it wasn't her fault I got away, 'cause I said I was going to see my other sister, but she said she'd be stricter. But Mrs. Christen said she didn't trust her anymore. She had me and my younger sister put with Mrs. Quadson to keep us from telling anyone what happened to my parents. But now it was too dangerous 'cause my older sister woke up and is trying to talk. So Mrs. Christen said she was goin' to split us up to keep us quiet. And she said if she had to, she'd send my big sister away and put my little sister in a different home." Tiffany was getting teary-eyed. "But if you adopt us, then she can't do anything."

A fire was growing in my stomach. I drew in a deep breath and looked out the window. Adopting these kids would be a big responsibility, but if I didn't adopt them, Amanda Christen could make their lives miserable.

I rubbed my face. "How old are your sisters?"

She perked up. "Tammy is five, Taylor is sixteen, and I'm eight."

I drummed my fingers on the table. Five, eight, and sixteen? Three girls? I had what I needed from her, and I owed her, but this was too big. Then I thought about Alexa and how she didn't like me taking advantage of this little girl. Ever since Tiffany met with me, things just kept getting worse for her and her sisters.

I looked at Tiffany. "What happened to your older sister? Why can't she take care of you?"

Tiffany looked down again. "She was in the accident that killed our parents . . . and she was hurt real bad. Ms. Rivera said she was in a coma an' she might not wake up. But even though she did wake up, Mrs. Christen . . ."

I sighed. Amanda would do anything to keep these three quiet. Tiffany and her story was probably the most powerful piece of evidence I had . . . or at least the most tear-jerking . . . she'd keep them from making things worse at all costs, even if it meant separating three orphaned sisters.

There wasn't anything else I could do. "All right, Tiffany. I'll do it."

Tiffany jumped up in her seat. *"Thankyouthankyou thankyoulpromisewewon'tbebad!!!"*

Something flashed in my mind's eye. It was too quick to really see what it was, but it had something to do with another little girl like Tiffany . . . it felt so familiar. To my surprise a lump grew in my throat and my eyes started to water. What was going on? Then I heard a soft voice, like an echo, that started to grow stronger but vanished when Tiffany grabbed me around the neck and hugged me tightly.

What just happened?

I shook the feeling off and swallowed the lump. I pulled Tiffany off and whispered to her. "Tiffany, before we get started, I need you to go back to Mrs. Quadson's house and get your sister. When you have her, run to the . . ."

She raised her eyebrows. "Yeah?"

I thought furiously about what I wanted her to do. She couldn't go anywhere the Christens or Quadson might think to look. "Go to the front wall at the edge of the city and hide in one of the corners. Wait there until Dieg—Mr. Rivera comes and gets you. Do you know who Mr. Rivera is?" I raised my eyebrows. "He's the bald guy with the big moustache."

She nodded again. "Yeah, I know him."

"Good. Wait for him there. Do not go with anyone else, even if they say they'll take you to him. Got it?"

She nodded furiously. "Got it."

I let her go and she ran out the door with the same conviction Alexa had. I sighed. I was going to need Alexa's help, but I knew she'd want me to do something in return. I grabbed my hat and hastily approached Mrs. Perchuni. She had been watching us.

"Mrs. P., I need to use your landline."

She nodded. "Got it." She escorted me to the back and left me to my call. I dialed Diego's office.

"Sí, this is—"

I whispered into the phone. "Diego, its Parker. I need you to do something and it is very important you do not tell anyone. Can I count on you?"

He scoffed over the line. "Of course, my friend, what do you need of me?"

*

I waited in the hospital lunchroom and waited for Alexa to take her lunch break. When she walked in, I flagged her down and bade her to sit with me.

"Mr. Parker? What are you doing here?"

I calmly glanced around and looked at her. "Do you remember what I wanted this morning? About the girl?"

Alexa shook her head. "Mr. Parker I will not help you—"

"I won't use her testimony."

She looked at me with a little confusion. "Really?"

I gestured to an empty chair. She sat. I leaned forward. "I need your help. If you do, I will take Tiffany's interview out of the trial."

She leaned forward. "What happened to change your mind?"

I glanced over my shoulder to make sure no one was within earshot. "Tiffany came to me earlier today and asked me a favor."

Alexa nodded. "Okay . . ."

"You are aware she has two sisters? A younger one and an older one here in the hospital? She asked me to adopt them."

Alexa raised her eyebrows. "What?"

I rubbed my forehead. "She told me Amanda was going to separate the three of them to keep them from talking. Amanda's seen what Tiffany's story did in rousing public support of this trial, so she's doing damage control."

She shook her head. "I . . . I can't believe she'd do something like that. Are you trying to get me to side with you for the court-martial? Because if you are—"

I looked at her with all of the seriousness in my being. "I am not lying, and I have decided I will do anything to keep them out of Amanda's reach. But I am going to need your help."

She looked at me, still not quite sure whether to believe me.

I leaned forward. "I've already sent Diego to collect Tiffany and her younger sister, Tammy, and have instructed him to meet with us in Taylor's room."

Alexa leaned back and thought quietly.

"Alexa . . . speak with her, listen to what she has to say. Then decide whether to believe me."

She nodded.

"Good. Let's go."

She looked up at me as I stood. "Now?"

I nodded. "I told Diego to move as quickly as possible. He's probably there now."

*

Alexa and I arrived at Taylor's room, and we paused when we heard voices inside.

"Do you understand the situation?"

"You can't do this . . ."

"Taylor . . . you have no idea what I can do."

Alexa and I stood at the cracked door and eavesdropped as Amanda blackmailed a young blonde woman who looked like an older version of Tiffany.

"This isn't right! Charlie was behind that accident, and you—"

Amanda raised her voice. "That is enough! Charlie wasn't anywhere near your parents, and you're going to do as I say. It'd be a pity if anything were to happen to your sisters."

Alexa surged into the room screaming at Amanda. "*Usted vaca sucia! ¿Cómo te atreves a hacerme esto a uno de mis pacientes? ¿Para esta pobre chica? ¡Amanda salir de aquí ahora mismo!*"

Amanda looked confused, insulted, and terrified all at once. She obviously had no idea what Alexa said, but it sounded bad, even to me. Then her attention was drawn to the doorway . . . where I stood leaning against the frame. I smiled and tilted my hat to her. Blood rushed to her face as it dawned on her that I was somehow behind Tiffany and

Tammy's vanishing act, and that I'd just made a critical ally by exposing her.

Amanda straightened up and composed herself before excusing herself from the room. I smiled as she passed me by, and even though I did not watch her leave, I could hear the sound of her frustration as her heels clicked down the hallway.

The rage instantly drained out of Alexa when she turned to Taylor. "*¡Oh, Dios mío! ¿Taylor, está bien? No puedo creer—*"

Taylor looked very confused but relieved at the same time. "Ah, Dr. Rivera? I can't understand . . ."

Alexa shook her head and walked to the girl. "I'm sorry, Taylor. What I said was, are you all right?"

Taylor flinched as she tried to sit up in bed. "Dr. Rivera, you can't tell anyone, but she said they have my sisters and—"

The doors in the hallway flew open, and suddenly the sound of three people running echoed down the corridors. I stepped aside as another pair of younger blonde girls burst into the room and rushed to Taylor.

"Taylor!"

"Tiffany?"

"Taylor!"

"Tam—"

Alexa caught Tiffany and Tammy before they jumped into her bed. She crouched low and looked them in the eyes. "I know you're glad to see her, but you cannot roughhouse yet. Taylor is still recovering from her head injury, and you can't agitate her sides because her ribs are still healing. You can hold hands, but you've got to be gentle . . . okay?"

Tiffany and Tammy nodded and rushed to their older sister's bedside. Alexa, Diego, and I all stood back as the sisters rejoiced each other's company. I pulled the two outside. "Diego, are you up to speed?"

Diego grinned and spoke in his normally loud voice but quickly quieted down when Alexa glared at him. "Yes, my friend, you've agreed to adopt them!"

I nodded. "That's basically the gist of the story, but has Tiffany told you about Amanda?"

Diego's face darkened. "Yes, she has. It appears there is more than one Christen who will need to be dealt with . . ."

Chapter 6—The Court-Martial

On the morning of the hearing I sat at my favorite outdoor café with a cup of black coffee and prepared for the ordeal as best as I knew how. But before I could take my first sip, a scrawny eight-year-old girl with dirty blonde hair appeared out of nowhere and hopped into the seat across from me.

She beamed at me through a light coat of freckles. "Hi, Mr. Parker!"

She started kicking her feet and shuffled some of my papers around. I lazily sipped the steamy coffee and watched people pass by. She was trying to annoy me . . . I repressed a smile.

It was little more than a month since I moved from my comfortable two-bedroom apartment to a larger four-bedroom so Tiffany and Tammy could come live with me, all in the pursuit of fitting the requirements to become the legal guardian to the three sisters. Or at least until Taylor was well enough to care for them herself. I hadn't really planned that far ahead. Anyway, it hadn't been completely unbearable . . . except for the occasional flashbacks to some forgotten memory whenever Tammy woke me up after a bad dream or Tiffany raided my private library and asked for a story.

I smiled. I hadn't had any progress in breaking that mental wall in weeks, so I let it be. Hopefully my sanity would return to normal and I would have an idea as to what the big deal was.

Tiffany looked at me quizzically. "Mr. Parker?"

I smiled and looked at her. "I'm sorry, Tiffany, I'm just a little lost in the clouds. Today's the big day, isn't it?"

She smiled widely. "Don't worry; you're gonna do good."

I smiled back. "How is Taylor doing? She still struggling?"

Tiffany's smile dampened a little. "Yeah . . . Mrs. Rivera says her legs will recover with some therapy and her head is going to be fine."

I messed her hair. "Must be tough for a kid your age to take care of your sisters by yourself."

She pushed my hand away and looked at me with the most stern expression she could muster. "Mr. Parker, I am nine years old. I am not a kid."

I smiled. "I'm sorry. Last time I checked you were still eight."

She looked away with a little huff. "Fine. But I might as well be nine; it's only two months to my next birthday."

I laughed and gathered my things. "I'm sorry, Tiffany, but I see anyone younger than twenty-five as a kid."

She grinned back. "Yeah, well, I'm surprised you can see anything at your age."

I dramatically grabbed my heart. "Oh! You wound me . . . I'm not that old; I'm not even forty . . . at least I don't think I am."

We poked fun at each other until I stood to leave for the courtroom. Then Tiffany became more somber. "Mr. Parker . . ."

"Yes?"

She looked at me with a grim expression. "Are you finally getting rid of Charlie?"

I knelt to her level. "Yes."

"Good."

*

As I opened the heavy wooden doors and entered the courtroom, I was greeted with the sound of a hundred of softly spoken conversations. The very air sparked with excitement as a crowd of two hundred plus eagerly awaited the trial of Charlie Christian. The room appeared to be modeled after the old US Supreme Court in Old Washington, with a raised winged bench where most of the council members would preside as judges. They would listen to the prosecution and the defense and then pass judgment without jury. But today Amanda wouldn't be acting as a judge. Navarro decided her relationship with Charlie might influence her decision, so she was barred from the bench. However, she was allowed to act as Charlie's defense.

When I reached my seat behind the prosecution desk, I set my things down and glanced around the room. In the crowd were familiar faces I recognized from my interviews and some I did not. I stopped when I spotted my competition entering from across the room to the defense desk.

Amanda sat stiff and angular in her chair, looking down at a small bundle of documents I assumed were manufactured. I smiled grimly. Charlie shouldn't have been the only one being tried for abusing power; all the Christens were guilty. Without another thought I took my seat and waited patiently for the council and Navarro to enter.

Five minutes later the crowd started to hush as a door to the back room opened and the council members entered. As usual, Sam and the mysterious Ms. Johnson were absent (probably opting to let Navarro Vote for them) and neither Alexa nor Diego would be acting as a judges. In total, five judges, plus Navarro, would preside.

Navarro took his seat last, and when he was comfortable, he signaled the bailiff to fetch Charlie. The bailiff left briefly before reappearing with Charlie and the three guards, Stevenson, Wesley, and Schwartz, who escorted him.

Charlie didn't have his defiant demeanor with him today. Instead, he was shifty-eyed and seemed panicked. His limp hair covered his boney scalp with a fine coat of sweat and oil. Dark circles surrounded his eyes, giving the impression they had sunk deeper into their sockets. It was apparent his own paranoid mind had tortured him while waiting for the trial. He jumped when Navarro struck the table with his gavel.

Navarro slowly scanned the room. "This examination has been called to determine if Charles Christen is fit to work on the security force." Navarro looked at Amanda and Charlie and spoke in a bored manner. "The defense has the opening statement."

Amanda got up, briefly glared at me, and walked to the middle of the floor. "This hearing today is not about my nephew but about the man who attacked him and is trying to save himself from punishment. I have the testimonies of several witnesses saying they watched the prosecutor repeatedly attack the defendant without cause." She looked at me. "That is all." Amanda walked back to her seat and sat.

Navarro nodded toward me. "The prosecution has the floor."

I stood and smiled warmly toward Amanda. "It goes without saying I disagree with the defense. Charlie is here because the people are tired of his injustices toward them. His victims have united and decided they will no longer be bullied or blackmailed—"

"I object!" Amanda shouted. "The prosecution is—"

Navarro lazily struck a block of wood with a gavel. "Overruled. Mr. Parker, you may continue."

I smiled and nodded. "Thank you. I stand before this trial to prove that Charles Christen, a.k.a. Charlie, abuses his power to harass and commit vandalisms against innocent citizens. I, along with many other individuals, have noticed a constantly escalating problem of paranoia, irrationality, and violence."

Amanda jumped out of her chair. "*I object!* The prosecution cannot make statements of—"

Navarro struck his gavel. "Overruled. Mr. Parker, you may continue."

I smiled. I could already see where this case was going. "Thank you. I have many statements from witnesses who have come forward to reveal incidents and grievances they were bullied into dropping. Many of these victims will discredit the defense's so-called 'witnesses' and expose a greater conspiracy aimed to protect the accused. Thank you."

The Christens presented statements and called witnesses to debunk my case and undermine my integrity. But when I took the stand, it became obvious the whole trial was fixed in my favor. Amanda became more and more frustrated as I continued to bring forth witnesses and victims who saw Charlie try to beat up an eleven-year-old kid because he was "annoying." I exposed sexual harassment incidents where Charlie tried forcing himself on women by flaunting a badge, a gun, and a threat of unwarranted investigation. He even put down two permitted pets because they were loose and "charged him." The list went on and got worse as I presented my testimonies and resubmitted complaint forms. But my coup de grâce was when I called Alexa to give a psychoanalytic report.

Navarro spoke. "Mrs. Rivera, you have submitted a general evaluation of the mental state of the defendant. Please read the key elements you've determined the defendant to exhibit."

After taking the stand, Alexa spoke prudently. "I believe Mr. Christen exhibits classic signs of bipolar disorder. My report lists various cases where the defendant has experienced forms of mania, which often led to incidents of anger, frustration, and violence toward others. The list includes . . ."

Alexa went on to clearly present several examples of Charlie's blatant misuse of power and violent confrontations, which Charlie didn't take very well. He had delusions of Alexa coming to his rescue and saving him from this completely *unfair* hearing. So when he heard her report, he looked shaken to his very core. During the rest of the trial Charlie looked pathetically for anyone to have pity and help him. Unfortunately, many of the council had already resolved to vote against Charlie. The rest of my presentation was simple and went smoothly.

Navarro struck his gavel. "Thank you, Mr. Parker. Does the defense have anything more to add? Do you have anything you wish to say, Mrs. Christen?"

Amanda sat with her hand covering her eyes while Charlie smiled in denial.

Navarro calmly looked around. "Very well. The council will discuss our decision in private and convene later when we has reached a verdict."

Navarro struck the desk with his gavel to officially end the hearing and swung his chair to leave.

But after that resounding *crack,* Charlie snapped back to reality and psychotically ran toward me. *"You motherfucker! You're not getting away with this! I'm gonna—"*

I didn't even acknowledge him. I just stepped out of Charlie's way, tripped him up, and sent him right into the wall. As soon as Charlie slid down, Stevenson, Wesley, and Schwartz were on him and started wrestling him out of the room. Everyone watched Charlie screaming insults at me and the council, except Navarro, who simply walked out of the room as Diego roared orders.

"¡Conseguir este bastardo de aquí!"

Navarro didn't even look up when Diego and his men disappeared into the hallway with Charlie. Charlie was nothing to him, just a simple dog barking from across the street.

*

When court was once again in session, the council voted Charlie was unfit to work as a guard, and he was convicted of dozens of accounts of vandalism, harassment, and violence and was sentenced to house arrest. From what I heard he kicked and screamed the entire time he was dragged to his room and for a long time afterward. In fact, I'm sure half the fort heard his howls of anger and frustration echoing up and down the hallways.

As I walked back to my apartment, my dark stalker appeared. "I'm willing to bet this isn't the last we're going to hear from our unbalanced friend."

I paused.

He smiled at me. "If you want my opinion, Charlie and his family are not going to take this lying down. They are going to do something to hurt everyone who betrayed them . . . and that may mean people are going to die."

*

After several weeks my fears were confirmed. It took twelve men, two hours, and many repeated warnings to break down the door of Charlie's downsized residence. Curiously, they discovered he wasn't there. Immediately afterward Diego had the entire police force search for Charlie, starting with the Christens' residence. But when it was discovered the Christens, along with two vehicles, were missing too, Navarro put the fort on lockdown. Eventually the entire fort was searched and no trace of anyone named Christen was found. After several weeks with no results, Navarro called off the search. The current theory was they left for the Badlands.

It was too much to hope they were gone for good.

Chapter 7—Time to Do Your Job

On a hot afternoon I enjoyed the cool shade of my favorite apple tree. Everything was right with the world. Taylor finally healed and Tiffany had both her sisters back. Taylor stepped up and took on the responsibilities of raising her sisters, and since I was still their lawful guardian, I checked in on them every other day.

I looked at the clear-blue sky above me. Clouds drifted lazily around the sun without a care in the world. A warm breeze blew my way as I thought about the joyful three months of cooking dinners, indulging tea parties, reading bedtime stories . . .

I frowned. I didn't know why it came naturally . . . as if I'd done those things before.

"Parker! *There* you are! I have looked *everywhere!*"

I jumped as Diego surprised me with his loud geyser of energy. "Diego . . . just when I thought I'd have time to myself."

Diego's brow furrowed. "Parker, I bring bad news. Communications in the solar farm has been offline for several days."

I yawned and stood to greet him. "What's that about a solar farm?"

Diego looked back a little confused. "Sí . . . due to increase of power consumption, a decommissioned solar farm west of here has been restored."

I raised my eyebrows. "When did *that* happen?"

Diego's worried mood broke and he cracked a wry smile. "You would have known this if you pay any attention during the meetings."

I gave a half-hearted laugh. "I'll take that under advisement. So that's the reason those cables along the rail car tracks are being reinforced."

Diego shook his head. "Parker . . ."

I raised my hands. "Right, right . . . so what about this new solar farm?"

Diego looked exasperated. "As I was saying, we are recommissioning and old solar farm to meet the rising demand in power—"

I scratched my head. "Where is this place again?"

Diego rubbed his forehead. "Ay-ay-ay-ay . . . once you exit the canyon, you will head directly west, and in about thirty miles you come across a dried river. Follow that north and you will find the farm ten miles from the tallest mountain. Any *more* questions?"

I let my shoulders drop. I hated the heat. "No worries. I'll send one of my runners."

Diego shook his head as I calmly reached for my water bottle. "This mission is too important to be trusted to a boy. We need a *man* with experience. Anyway, your runners have reported an increase of walkers, and there is speculation they might not be able to handle such a task."

I rolled my eyes and began to sip some water. "Fine . . . I'll go."

Diego smiled and nodded. "Good. Now . . . you will be traveling by horse, so this will most likely be a day or two journey."

I coughed up my mouthful of water. "A horse! What happened to my usual Ford?"

Diego shrugged. "We've been having problems finding replacement parts for our vehicles, so the council has decided to spare them for more drastic *problemas*."

I thought for a moment. "What about that dirt bike one of my runners found a few weeks ago?"

It was Diego's turn to be alarmed. "*¿Qué?* Parker, he pulled that thing out of a garage two weeks ago! Our mechanics haven't even looked at it yet!"

I shook my head. "It's so hard to find good help. Can't they just give it a once over?"

Diego looked worried. "Parker . . ."

I gave him a sincere smile. "Tell the boys to skip the spinning rims and just test the engine."

Diego shook his head before smiling. "Very well, Parker, if you insist."

My smile evolved into a grin. "Great, what next?"

Diego nodded. "Yes. We are in the middle of a drought, so take plenty of water."

I thought for a moment. "Aren't we in the rainy season?"

Diego nodded again. "*Sí*, that brings up another *problema*. Watch the weather and be mindful of flash floods. I suggest you do not travel along the riverbed."

I looked at the darkening horizon. "I suppose this won't be so bad. I *am* starting to feel a little anxious behind the fort walls. Maybe a run outside will help ease my restlessness."

Diego laughed and slapped my back. "Very *good!* Get ready . . . enjoy the company of a beautiful woman, and say your prayers . . . you leave early tomorrow morning."

*

I was at the main gate long before the sun rose.

I was telling the truth when I told Diego I was restless behind these steel and cement walls. Even this rudimentary assignment seemed like a good way to escape the monotony. I barely noticed how I repeatedly checked if my knife and hatchet were secured in their sheaths as I walked to the gates. Then again, they were very important. The sharpened cold blades made wonderful companions.

And when the side door was finally opened I made another quick mental inventory check. My hatchet was on my left hip and my knife was horizontally secured along the base of my back. I also carried a Webley-Fosbery automatic revolver on my right hip. I had my favorite "Eastwood" hat, one very comfortable poncho, two gallons of water in a travel bladder, twenty feet of spelunking rope, one small supply of pork jerky, one compass, one grenade, one lighter, and twenty-four rounds of ammunition for my revolver. Yup, that sounded right; time to go.

I descended the steps to the loading platform where the train and its new conductor waited to take me through the canyon.

*

The cool air swirled through the tram as it made its way to the entrance of the dark canyon. I looked out the tram's open door and saw the full moon hanging in the dark night like a bright fluorescent pearl.

The silence broke as the conductor spoke up. "It's pretty, isn't it?"

I turned to the conductor, who stood at the tram's speed controls. She smiled at me awkwardly and I smiled back. "Yeah, I suppose it is . . . do you know how much longer until we reach the ranch?"

She nodded. "We're almost there now. It's just around this next bend."

True to her word, the canyon's entrance appeared as we rounded a turn. About a hundred feet from the end of the tracks the tram slowed from its comfortable cruise of twenty miles per hour until it finally stopped. When she gave the "all clear," I grabbed my travel bag and stepped down to the cement platform.

She leaned out the door before I started down the steps and waved to me. "Good luck, Mr. Parker!"

I waved back. "See you around."

She smiled and went back to the controls. In a few moments the tram slowly moved down the tracks back to the fort. I watched it gather speed and eventually disappear out of sight. I sighed, hitched my bag higher on my shoulder, and descended down the thirty-three steps to the canyon floor, where Sam waited for me.

He stood next to his favorite horse and sported a wide smile. "Howdy, Parker! I hear y'alls makin' a long trip."

I grinned back. "Yup, is the bike ready?"

Sam patted the dark brown muzzle of a good-looking mare with a light tan coat. "I saw that wreck when them mechanic boys pushed it here. Y'all sure ya don' want a horse? They're more reliable."

I let my travel bag slide to the ground. "I'm sure your horses are first class, Sam, but I want speed on this trip."

Sam chuckled. "I don't know if that's what you're gettin', Parker."

I watched a couple of men wheel the bike over to us. Diego was right . . . that wreck didn't inspire much confidence. I picked up the helmet and put my hat in my travel bag.

I smiled and shook my head. "Ah well, what's life without a little gamble?"

*

It was very hot. The sun was already high in the sky and I *still* hadn't come across the river. Christ . . . it had to be a hundred degrees. Good thing I had water.

I looked along the horizon, hoping to spot something before being surprised by a dark figure on a black dirt bike in an all-black dirt bike costume riding up to me.

I heard his voice even though I shouldn't. "Reminds me of the old days when it was just you an' me."

I shifted my eyes away from him. Damn. He was here. "Nice outfit. You're not going to last long with that black uniform."

He grinned back at me with a crooked smile. "Yeah, but you got to admit it looks cool. I originally thought about riding a fiery horse's skeleton, 'cause you keep callin' me a phantom, but I decided it was a little too trick or treat."

I drew in a breath of hot prairie air and sighed. "This is going to be a long ride."

He nodded, pretending to understand. "Maybe . . . but—"

I cut him off as my front wheel fell into an invisible trench and I was launched forward. I bounced along the ground three times before rolling to a stop on a patch of dried curled mud. I turned over and lay flat on the ground to wait for the world to stop spinning. As I stared up at the blazing sun, I couldn't help but dread the pain from skipping on the ground like a pebble on a lake.

The man in black pulled up and looked down on me with a cruel smile. "You all right?"

I shifted my eyes from the bright sky to the man in black. "Peachy."

He chuckled and looked at the distance between me and the bike. "That was pretty cool. You looked like a ragdoll thrown by a toddler."

"Fuck you."

He shook his head. "Those sandpits can be a real bitch. Can you move, or are you gonna bake in the sun like a cartoon egg?"

I slowly moved my legs toward me before moving my arms. Everything hurt, but nothing seemed broken. I pushed myself up and sat for a moment. My back was okay . . . if not a little sore. I stood and dusted myself before looking at the damage. My pants and shirt were torn beyond recognition, my poncho disappeared, and my pack was gone. Blood started to seep from each tear. I must have lost a lot of skin if I couldn't feel those scrapes. I pulled off my helmet and rolled my neck . . . nothing too bad there either.

After an hour of gathering my things, repeatedly failing at restarting my bike, and enduring the phantom's prattling, I decided to try and walk the rest of the way. Unfortunately, it was another three hours before I finally found the riverbed.

With a deep breath of scorching dry air, I climbed down with stiff legs, stretched, and drank the last bit of my water. I had to leave an entire gallon of water and half of my other supplies after abandoning my broken bike. I could only bring my hat, my weapons, ten scraps of my poncho I sacrificed for bandages, and a gallon of water-scrap that, an empty gallon jug. I looked along the riverbed for water. Even a hot, gritty, muddy puddle would be great. I sighed and let my shoulders drop. Unfortunately there were no puddles to be seen.

With a quick shake of my head I snapped out of my disappointment. "Which way is north? Diego said that once I hit the river, head north. Hmmm . . ."

The stalker dismounted his make-believe bike and followed me. "Hold on, Evel Knievel . . . I know what you're thinking. Don' you remember Diego said it's a bad idea to ride in the riverbed?"

I ignored him. The riverbed was smooth and I could make great time walking it. I just had to keep an eye on the sky.

After it reached midday I started to worry I overshot the farm.

My stalker rode his bike in circles around me. "Yeah, that would be a problem . . . wait! There it is! Looks like we didn't—"

I paused. "Crap."

He paused too. "Ditto."

As we—I—climbed out of the riverbed, I paused. I found the solar farm, but instead of relief, a pit formed in my stomach. Surrounding the compound was maybe fifty or more walkers frantically searching for an entrance. A gust of wind blew my scent in their direction, and it didn't take long for them to smell my blood. In an almost uniform motion they turned toward me. I pulled out my gun and stood my ground.

My stalker rode up beside me with an impressed expression. "What do you think you're doin'?"

I ignored him and glanced at the sun. It was midday . . .
the sun wouldn't set until seven or eight. If I was going to fight,
now was the time.

The man in black took off his helmet and raised his
eyebrows. "I'm sorry, did you think silently to yourself you are
going to fight?"

"I'm injured. There is no way to outrun these creatures,
and even if I could run, I'd be at risk of heat stroke. The only
option is to make a stand and fight now while I have the energy."

My stalker jumped from his bike as it evaporated into
thin air and walked to me. "Sounds like a plan, but these plans
are never that simple."

I looked at him from the corner of my eye. "Only thing I
can think of."

He smiled. "Well, the bright side is, I won't have to put
up with you if you die."

I turned back to the charging infected. As I expected, a
dozen or more walkers outran the rest of the mob.

I started muttering to myself to clear my mind. "The
fence surrounding the compound isn't made to hold back so
many of those things. It will collapse soon if I don't do something
now . . . . And if those things storm the compound . . . well, the
fort will lose a lot of scientists and technicians. It's part of my
job to prevent something like that."

I fired two rounds as the creatures neared me. I nailed
the lead walker in the head and shoulder. When he collapsed I
climbed down a steep part of the riverbank. I stopped and faced
them as they leapt after me. It was easy to thrust my knife and
slam my axe through their skulls. In a relatively short amount
of time, it was over and they were dead.

Unfortunately, that was just the prelude. Nearly all of them started running toward me.

The second wave started badly and dragged on for too long and eventually ended up under the forest of solar panels. They charged in a singular wave, those mindless monsters. Their rotting, infected bodies overwhelmed my senses with a stench that filled my nose and crawled down my throat like a ravenous rat. I fought through teary eyes while trying to keep from retching.

It was hard. Any other man would have died by now . . . but I knew how to fight them. First, get them separated. Make them run. It's during the chase they will naturally spread out due to the varying decay of their bodies. Then they can be fought one-to-five instead of one-to-twelve. Second, wear thick clothing or armor, which will make it harder for them to get at the skin if they get close enough to bite. Third, fight with a knife or any other kind of blade, only use a gun as a last resort and only if there's a clear shot of the head or heart; anywhere else won't do crap. If the head or heart are destroyed, they'll almost instantly freeze as the blood in their veins coagulates.

After forty minutes I was able to kill at least thirty of these things with my axe, knife, and revolver. Still . . . running and fighting was extremely exhausting, especially when combined with the afternoon heat, dehydration, and existing injuries. Eventually my strikes became weaker and my shots sloppy.

"I don't think I'll last much longer . . . got to fall back . . ."

I hobbled to the shade of one of the solar panels and collapsed to the ground. Five walkers charged in a disorganized group. I stripped off my backpack and dug around for my grenade. When I had it in hand, I pulled the pin and chucked it at them. In a couple of beats the small group evaporated as their bodies were shredded by the shrapnel and explosion. I paused and watched as a lone foot flew from the detonation and hit another walker twenty feet away. I tried not to be impressed and went back to gathering the rest of my bullets. I loaded them in my gun.

If I live through this, I'd better thank Diego for the gun. I looked down at my hand. "Damn . . ."

I only had three bullets left . . .

Bam! Bam! BAM!

There they went, and I didn't hit anything.

There were at least five more . . . "Can't get up . . ."

At least the last few were skeletonized, starved, and scabby. These guys were the ones who couldn't keep up with the main flock during the beginning of the fight.

Damn . . . that one is getting too close . . . I need to get up.

The man in black materialized and crouched beside me. "You're lookin' pretty pathetic."

I leaned my head toward him and choked out a few words. "This isn't the time . . ."

He looked around. "Incoming."

I raised my knife and let a walker run right into it. I got lucky and it went through its heart. Unfortunately, it got stuck as the coagulating blood cemented my knife in the dead walker's chest.

I pushed it aside and grinned as the last four limped to me. "Looks like this is it . . ."

He put a hand on my shoulder. "I just want to let you know . . . I really enjoyed tormenting you."

Everything started to darken. "Right . . ."

"Come on, there are only four of them! Get them before they bite him."

I regained consciousness when I heard a woman's voice. My head started to throb and every move I tried to make was a struggle against gravity.

What am I doing here? I was . . . I was . . . holy crap! What the hell happened?

I sprang up and saw ten techs sloppily firing at the walkers with shotguns. Almost instantly I felt a head rush and fell backward. Cool . . . looked like I wasn't gonna die.

I blinked and the dark figure appeared over me with a wicked grin. "Wow, you are probably the luckiest bastard on the planet."

I frowned and slowly shook my head. "What?"

He smiled. "When you passed out, a couple of guys actually grew a pair."

I blinked slowly and looked at the metal beams of the solar panel above me. "What?"

He nodded. "Someone did your job for you."

I fruitlessly tried to stand. "We should probably try to find our way into the compound. They'll have food and water . . ."

The phantom started to walk away. "Good plan . . . go ahead. I'll meet you inside."

I stopped trying to sit up. "Can't move."

"Excuse me?"

I yelled as best as I could. *"Hey! I'll get up when I can!"*

"Sir . . . are you feeling all right?"

I paused. *"What?"*

90

I tilted my head and squinted with difficulty to see a woman with long black hair in what looked like a white lab coat. I tried focusing, but seeing was getting harder by the minute. Then something occurred to me . . . when did I stop talking to the guy in my head and start talking to her?

She looked worried. "Are you from the fort?"

I closed my eyes. "Yes."

*

I woke up dazed and confused. The first thing I recognized was a throbbing headache. I blinked to clear my vision and slowly scanned the room. From what I could tell, I was in a hospital bed in a recovery ward. My makeshift bandages had been removed and my wounds redressed, and my right arm had a needle leading to an IV drip sticking out of it, and I was wearing an oxygen mask.

Someone with a smooth voice spoke. "Good, you're awake."

I shifted my vision to my left.

A woman waved her hand to get my attention and smiled. "Over here."

I gazed at her. I thought that was the woman I briefly met outside. I spoke through the mask with a raspy voice. "Where am I?"

She stood and pulled something out of her pocket. "You are at the Desierto Grande Solar Farm."

It hurt to think. "What?"

She leaned over me and flashed a light in my eyes. "Translation: The Big Solar Farm. I know, the name hits you on the nose, but that's what you get when a Mexican is in charge."

I blinked. "Oh . . . guess I made it."

She put her light away. "So you *are* from the fort."

"Yes."

She smiled . . . she had a great smile. My vision started to clear and I began to take in what was around me. She was the woman I saw earlier . . . she was very beautiful. Sunlight shined off supple, snow-white skin and reflected off pitch-black hair worn in a bun with even bangs that hung over her forehead. From what I could tell, her body was *very* well proportioned, but it was her flawless, sharp, sapphire-blue eyes that really caught my attention. Right then and there I could tell those eyes would be my salvation . . . or my downfall.

She gently put her fingers on my wrist and felt for the pulse in my radial artery. "You haven't passed out again? Have you?"

I sighed quietly. "No, I'm still here."

She mockingly cocked an eyebrow. "Good. Then you're just undressing me with your eyes."

I smiled weakly. "Wow, beautiful and smart."

She pulled out an old digital blood-pressure cuff. "My name is Heloise Johnson. Can you tell me who you are?"

I thought for a moment. "Heloise Johnson? Aren't you the power manager for the fort?"

She nodded as she wrapped the blood-pressure cuff around my arm. "I am, and I'm also currently the head physician for this power station. Now, can you tell me who you are?"

I paused as the cuff inflated and started taking my blood pressure. "I'm the head runner, Parker."

Heloise looked at the cuff's readings and wrote them down on a clipboard. "Parker? Ahhh, you're Diego's new delivery boy."

I smiled and started to pull off the stuffy oxygen mask. "I prefer the title errand runner . . . not that I'm complaining, but why are you treating me?"

Without looking she lightly slapped my wrist and then recentered my mask. "Like I said, I am the current head physician, or rather, the normal doctor is . . . indisposed. So I am taking over his duties."

I blinked groggily still processing what she was saying. "You're a doctor too?"

She nodded and adjusted the IV drip. "Everyone needs a hobby. Oh, and you're welcome."

I raised my eyebrows. "What?"

She cocked an eyebrow. "When you passed out, who do you think took out the last of those creatures and brought you in?"

I looked at the ceiling and then back at her. "That was you?"

She briefly looked at me. "Well . . . no, but I gave the order."

I started to chuckle but winced when my ribs ached. "But I did see you out there, right?"

She set down her clipboard. "So you *were* conscious."

I nodded.

She flashed a smile. "I did make sure you hadn't been infected . . . or died."

I looked at her seriously. "Then thank you. I'm glad you were worried enough to come see me."

She looked down and brushed her bangs from her eyes. "You're welcome . . . would you like something to eat?"

I nodded. "Yes, and preferably something solid."

Her devious smile returned again. "Too bad, you're severely dehydrated and are suffering from heatstroke. You'll stay here and eat out of an IV drip until I say so. We can discuss why you're here when I decide you're feeling better."

I laughed. "Wouldn't that be my call?"

She put her hand on her hip. "Nope, I'm your doctor. It's my call. Good-bye, Parker, see you soon."

I watched her shapely body walk smoothly through the doors. Then I looked up at the ceiling and watched the white room turn orange as the light of the sunset shined through the window. Then I fell asleep.

Chapter 8—Almost Dying Isn't That Bad

Diego arrived the day after the phone lines were re-established with half the fort's assault force. But when he heard of my full-scale battle with fifty walkers I could tell he was ecstatic when he heard I took them all on by myself. He wanted to bring me a drink and have me give him the play by play, but Heloise put her foot down and shooed him back to the fort as soon as the farm was secure.

She kept me in bed for two more days and restricted my diet to a tasteless slop with "all the essential vitamins." If I didn't know better, and I'm not saying I do, I'd say she was doing it all to annoy me. Anyway, on the fifth day she released me and finally allowed me to have a real lunch at a table.

Heloise sat with a glass of milk as I wolfed down a burger and chugged a tall glass of apple juice. "Well . . . what can I say? One day we're running some routine checks on the power output and out of the blue it shuts down. It was only after you saved us from two hundred walkers that we discovered the main power line was dug up, cut in half."

I smiled. "Two hundred?"

She rolled her eyes. "You know I am exaggerating, but it might as well have been a thousand. This complex doesn't have the means to defend itself against an onslaught like that. The people here are engineers, not fighters. We have some weapons, but the men and women here aren't trained well enough to use them effectively. I've tried to convince Navarro and his council of sniveling sheep that we need competent armed forces stationed out here, but they are all convinced that the station is safe because it's in the middle of a desert. Every time I bring the subject up, they argue nothing will ever reach us without dying of exposure."

I paused to swallow. "Good thing I had a bike."

Heloise cocked an eyebrow. "Of course. As I was saying, since the event last week, the council have to take my dema— ahem, *requests*, seriously."

I set my burger down and wiped my hands with a napkin. "Understandable, there hasn't been a group that large in more than a year."

Heloise leaned back in her chair and caressed her bottom lip with a finger. "Speaking of which, where could they have come from?"

I drank some juice and winced as I bumped one of my bandaged scrapes on the table. "I don't know, but they must have been wandering around for quite a while."

Heloise looked back up at me. "Really? How could you tell?"

I set my drink down and leaned back in my chair. "It's the way their bones were exposed. If I had to guess, they probably haven't had anything to eat in weeks. Did you say the main power line was dug up and cut in half?"

Heloise gave a small nod. "Yes, the power was off at the time for a routine check, so anyone could easily have cut it."

I furrowed my eyebrows. "I see."

Heloise looked at me intently. "Is there something on your mind, Parker?"

I looked into space. "Yeah . . . but it could be nothing. Several months ago an unbalanced guard was tried and found guilty of abusing his power. He disappeared later along with his only relatives and we haven't heard anything from him since."

Heloise looked at me intently. "You're talking about Charlie, aren't you?"

I nodded

Heloise looked annoyed. "I remember that scrawny little psychopath."

I chuckled. "Charlie's mind is a bag of cats. Anyone with any common sense could smell the crazy on him."

"You know . . . he once tried to force himself on me. The only reason he only got away with a limp was that old hag Amanda and her whimpering brother stepped in and bribed me not to say anything."

I cocked an eyebrow. "Bribed?"

She smiled shrewdly. "Yeah, half of their combined wages for two months."

I looked at her a little confused. "What could you want with so much cash? The fort provides everyone with equal access to resources."

She shrugged. "Montana is not a communist commune, there are things I want that cost more than the average wage provides. One can never have enough." She leaned back and waved me off. "Anyway, I'm sure Charlie and his auntie would do anything get back at Navarro and the fort. But I'm not sure how they could sic those creatures on us . . ."

I ate a few bites and thought for a moment. This was a real problem . . . if the Christens had figured out how to manipulate those things . . .

I looked around. Maybe thirty other people in the lunchroom were are on lunch breaks, dreading the beginning of a shift or enjoying the end of one. All these good people could have been killed because something or someone led those monsters here.

Heloise snapped her fingers. "Parker . . . I would like to discuss something else that happened the other day."

I snapped back to reality. "Oh?"

She brushed a few bangs away from her face and looked deep into my eyes. "I can't get something out of my mind . . ."

I started to feel uneasy. "What's that?"

Heloise started tapping the table with a perfectly manicured fingernail. "That day when you showed up . . ." Her sharp blue eyes were completely focused only on me. "You were cut all to hell, had heatstroke, and were alarmingly dehydrated, yet you managed to kill more than fifty of those creatures in triple-digit temperatures."

I smiled. "Your point?"

She smiled and narrowed her eyes. "How were you able to do that? I've never seen anyone able to pull something like that off . . . it was absolutely . . . *incredible*."

I lowered my burger and leaned forward. "Well . . . if you need to know . . . I'm secretly Superman."

She rolled her eyes. "I'm serious, no ordinary person could survive an onslaught like that."

I shrugged. "I wanted to live, nothing more, nothing less."

Heloise's eyes lit up. "That reminds me! I know what's causes the infection!"

I froze. "What?"

Heloise grinned. "Yeah, some time ago Mrs. Rivera sent some notes describing her discoveries regarding the bacterial nature of the infection."

I leaned forward. "And?"

Heloise sipped her drink. "Yes. The little princess finally got off her high horse and accepted she couldn't figure out what causes the infection. So she handed the project over to me."

I tilted my head. "Aren't you the manager here?"

She shrugged. "It's more like a hobby. Anyone can run this place. I'm only here because Navarro can't stand me but knows I'm too valuable to fire. So I've been banished to this cushy job."

I grinned. "You can actually get a rise out of Navarro?"

She waved me off. "It isn't that hard. Anyway, as you almost certainly know, their blood clots instantly after it stops moving. After I figured out how to keep the infected blood from congealing and turning all the organs into dried glue, I learned the muertos agitados are constantly producing vast amounts of adrenaline, dopamine, hydrocortisone, and another chemical I'd been unable to categorize. When I realized what gives them their nearly endless strength and stamina, I went directly to the adrenal glands. But before I could biopsy them, I discovered they were surrounded by a thick black covering and had swelled to massive sizes. When I dissected one of them, I learned an odd bacteria colony had virtually taken over and turned off the shut-off switch."

I leaned forward. "What can you take away from this information? Is there any way to find a cure?"

Heloise frowned. "As of now, no. I've tried various formulas and combinations of antibiotics, but none of the test subjects have survived so far."

I frowned. "What? What do you mean by test subjects?"

Heloise shrugged. "I have someone who captures test subjects for me for a fair price. So I may use them for experiments."

I pushed my food aside. "That is very dangerous for you and for everyone here."

She swirled her drink. "I take the proper precautions. And I can recognize how long a subject has been infected, so I don't buy anything I suspect he infected intentionally."

I frowned. "There are no proper precautions."

Heloise grinned maliciously. "Yes there are, you just need a certain amount of cruelty."

I put my hand over my mouth and thought deeply.

She glanced at me over her glass, trying to get a bead on what I was thinking. "Are you going to say something, Parker?"

I looked back at her. "Leon Trotsky said, 'The end may justify the means as long as there is something that justifies the end.' By that he meant doing something important does not give anyone the right to do something wrong."

Heloise smiled. "I am impressed . . . how about, 'I have laid a line that I will not cross . . . as long as there is someone willing to hold me back.'"

We smiled at each other. As soon as the landline to the fort was operational, I contacted Diego to let him know things were returning to normal and I'd been told the main power line would be repaired within a month. I also decided to take a small "vacation" (but really just wanted to spend more time with Heloise).

*

By nature I suppose I'm like a cat—I'm lazy and would prefer to find a high-up place, lie down in the shade of an apple tree, and just enjoy the quiet. Sometimes I would go off and hang out with some friends, work out, or work on a small project, but I enjoyed doing little to nothing. On the other hand, Heloise needed something to do all the time. She was the most interesting little minx I had ever met. She had the odd ability of being kind and friendly while at the same time being heartlessly cruel. She was beautiful, headstrong, smart, and a borderline psychopath . . . and that was what I liked about her (and everyone else hated).

I spent several more days enjoying those qualities, until a lanky man came running toward our table.

I narrowed my eyes as I noticed the panic in his. Something was wrong. "M-M-Mrs. *Juh-Juh-Johnson!* Mr. *P-Parker!*"

Heloise frowned. "*Brian!* Quit stammering and tell me what's wrong."

I couldn't help but smile at how easily Heloise could jump into work mode.

The man stopped and tried to keep his voice down. "So-so-sorry t-to inter-ru-ru-ru-rupt you M-M-Ms. Juh-Johns-son, b-but we-we-we . . . we j-just got a m-m-m-m-message fr-from Dee-Diego."

Heloise crossed her arms and frowned. "And? That doesn't sound like a reason to get worked up."

Brian couldn't keep it in anymore. "Mr. Diego has sent out distress code ten!"

The room went silent. Any code over seven meant a potential fort-wide infection . . . a code ten was very bad.

I stood. "I'm going back."

Heloise sprang up from her seat. "*What?* Parker, from what we can tell, the entire fort could be infected! Even if you could cross the prairie to the fort, it's not like you can go inside the *front door* without being torn apart. I doubt even you could survive fighting more than ten thousand of those creatures."

I turned to her. "Yeah . . . even I'm not crazy enough to pull off a stunt like that. I think I'll use the back door on the other side of the mountain."

Heloise slapped her forehead. "A rear entrance . . . at least tell me you have a plan."

A wide smile spread across my face. "Sorry, but that's not my style."

Heloise stared at me intently before rubbing her eyes. "All right, Parker, let's go."

"Wait, you—"

"Yes, Parker I am going, and if you don't like it, *you* can go to hell."

I looked away and scratched the back of my head. "Actually, I was thinking—"

Heloise rolled her eyes. "Please . . . don't think. I already know how we're going to get there."

I looked at her quizzically. She smiled, and in a split-second she took off and ran out of the cafeteria and down a hallway. I jumped to my feet and followed.

She glanced back at me. "Go get your things!"

I slid to a stop. "Where are *you* going?"

"To the station's garage, darling. I keep my baby there."

I was really confused. "Baby?"

When I had my things and finally caught up to her at the garage, she was slowly walking around a covered car.

In a flash she grabbed the tarp and pulled it off in one yank. "Let me present my custom VW chassis Dune Buggy"— she paused for effect—"with four cylinders, a four-speed manual shift, and a beautiful, silver fiberglass body. I spent years collecting the parts and restoring them."

I looked at the car and back to her. "You're a mechanic too?"

She smiled. "Everyone needs a hobby. Anyway, the hardest part was converting the engine to use propane instead of gasoline."

I was mesmerized by her ingenuity. "Propane?"

She stylishly vaulted into the driver's seat. "Get in and I'll explain."

I barely heard Heloise's explanation as we flew over rocks and dunes. She ran her buggy into jumps, skids, and drifts, all at insane speeds. If it wasn't for my seatbelt I would have been bucked out of the vehicle at least five times. The terrain finally evened out when Heloise dropped the buggy into the dry riverbed and started to follow it north to the rear entrance of the fort.

I gripped the door handle and the dashboard for dear life. *"Heloise, can't we slow down?"*

Heloise was focused on the terrain in front of us. "Can't! We need to find a way to the other side before the river floods and we die horribly!"

I looked up. She was right. The sky was getting darker, the wind was picking up speed, and everything was getting much colder. In maybe an hour the clouds would gather in such mass that the water molecules would accumulate to form rain. And because this was a desert, the rain that fell here was going to be heavy and fast. I didn't know how long until the riverbed filled with monsoon-powered runoff. I wondered if Heloise was aware of the extreme—

A knot formed in my stomach as an enormous wall of water appeared around the next bend and raced toward us.

In seconds we'd be thrashed, crushed, spun, smashed, and drowned under the immense power of a desert flood. I closed my eyes and braced myself for the impact when I suddenly pitched right. Heloise turned left and hit a naturally formed ramp and flew twenty feet before landing on the opposite shore.

When my eyes finally popped open and I could peel my hands off the dash, I looked around. On my right was a gigantic river flowing violently and angrily down the previously parched riverbed, and on my left was Heloise, looking amused at my very apparent fear.

I turned and glared at her. *"I never want to do that again!"*

Heloise grinned. "Don't be such a scaredy-cat; my baby here can handle anything."

I raised my finger at her. "Heloise, I—"

She hit the brakes and cut me off. "There's the mouth of the canyon!"

I looked around. Sam and his animals were gone, probably off toward the mountain pass he was so fond of. Except . . .

At that moment, the air and ground around us started exploding as two of the sentry stations opened fire on us. Heloise peeled out and headed for the hidden ramp.

She whipped her head around as the Hotchkiss cannons repeatedly launched exploding projectiles at us. "What the hell is going on? Why are they firing on us?"

I shook my head. "I'm more worried about who's firing those things!"

She looked at me while narrowly missing an exposed boulder. "What?"

I looked back as we drove out of range. "Didn't you notice!? There aren't any walker bodies at the mouth of the canyon, but the guns still work!"

Heloise grimly looked back at the path in front of us. "Someone took over the stations! Otherwise there would be corpses everywhere!"

I nodded and then looked up the mountain. "Drive around the bend there. In around a hundred feet is the ramp that leads to the back door."

The buggy's engine roared as Heloise spun next to the rear entrance. The path was difficult to see, but it was easy to recognize when one knows the landmarks.

I immediately unbuckled my seat belt and made to jump out when the buggy skidded to a stop. "As soon as I'm on the trail, get the he—"

Heloise grabbed my shirt and pulled me into a passionate kiss. She held on to my shirt and yelled over the howling wind, "Take this! Oh, and *don't die!*" She handed me a small package. "Use this just in case!"

I looked at it as she handed it to me. "What is it?"

She grinned mischievously. "A small amount of dynamite. It'll guarantee an explosive entrance!"

I tucked it in my bag. "Well . . . just in case the door sticks . . ."

She shrugged. "Whatever!" She yanked me in for another kiss and shoved me out of the buggy. "Get *moving!*"

I winced as my bruises hit rocks and my cuts threatened to reopen. To keep moving I muttered a motivating mantra. "One foothold after another, one grip after the other. Can't stop, I can't stop."

I stopped as I climbed over the last bolder and found my original campsite. It had been more than a year since Id last been here, and nearly all distinctive features had been blown away. It's possible I might have completely overlooked it if not for the circle of stones I'd used as my campfire. I smiled as I noticed the old crevasse. I paused to draw my gun then crossed the deteriorating campsite and walked inside. It was too dark to see anything, so I raised my free hand as I blindly walked, trying to feel for the hidden door. A while back this door let me know Montaña existed and helped me find it. With a flash and a reverberating *BOOM!*, the sky lit the inside of the crevasse. When everything went dark again the hairs on my neck rose for a moment.

The door was already open.

I heard a familiar voice. "That can't be good . . ."

I started moving again. "No."

I stepped through the door and into a pitch-black cement hallway. When I reached the end of a narrow hallway, I came to another unlocked, reinforced door. I jerking the door open. A couple of women screamed as I jumped inside a lit room gun-first and swung it around. As my eyes adjusted I saw the terrified faces of the council members and their immediate family members.

I heard the shaky voice of an old man. "P-P-Parker?" It was Mr. Turk, head of the small businesses. "W-Wh-Wha-"

I raised my free hand and holstered my gun. "Don't worry. I'm here to help."

Some of the women and children huddled against their fathers or grandfathers. I looked around. "Wait . . . where's Navarro? And where are Alexa and Matthew?"

Mrs. Price spoke up. "They're with the others in the main bunker. Do you know what's going on?"

I started to a door across the room. "I have a general idea."

Mrs. Price spoke a little angrily this time. "You need to stay here and protect us!"

I frowned at her before unlocking the door and running out.

*

I followed yet *another* long hallway before coming to another hidden door that led to the council's private dining room. I ran inside, downstairs, and through hallways until I finally arrived at a walkway overlooking the plaza. Then I stopped and stared, not able to fully comprehend what I was seeing. The infected were everywhere!

Emergency sirens wailed over screams of people being torn apart to sate the endless hunger of the walkers. Bloody footprints dotted the streets as walkers ran after the fort's civilians. I averted my eyes as a man and woman were cornered and suddenly torn apart by ten walkers. But wherever

I turned, people were screaming or crying in panic as they were being chased down the streets or pinned to the ground.

I jumped onto a handrail and rode it down to the ground. In less than a second the very air became soaked with water as rain came down like a waterfall. With a scream and a rush of adrenaline, I ran through the rain to the most concentrated pocket of walkers. Twenty feet away I drew my gun and screamed at them to get their attention. I shot ten dead, and as they charged me I holstered my gun and began slicing and stabbing everything in my path. I whooped and yelled as loudly as possible to get the attention of everything within earshot.

I wanted every crazed walker to know I was here so they would come to me instead of going after anyone else caught in their path, and when all their attention was on me, I ran. Always on the defensive and always moving. Never surrounded, stabbing through hearts, slicing throats, splitting heads, breaking joints—I had to keep moving. I *must keep moving.*

Christ, I'm on the ground! *Get up! Get up!* Get up!

My phantom appeared at my side as I got up and started running again. "This looks really dangerous."

I yelled at him but didn't lose focus. "You don't thi—"

Bam!

Bam!

Bam!

Ratatatatatatatatatata

Bam!

Bam!

Bam!

Ratatatatatatatatatata

I whirled around. "Guns! Someone's shooting. Who's shooting? *Behind me!*"

In my trail of carnage, Diego and thirty other men outfitted in riot gear rushed onto the battlefield with guns, *big* guns. Where the hell were they?

I yelled over the sound to the firing guns, the pounding rain, and the howling wind. "Diego! What the hell happened?"

Diego jogged up to me. "Later, my friend. Right now we need to close the main gate!" Diego turned and yelled at his men, *"¡Ir al infierno maldito hijos de puta!"*

I turned to the gates with disbelief. "Who the fuck opened the gates!"

Up ahead the walkers swarmed through the open main gates. Some of Diego's men were trying to shoot back the onslaught and close the gates, but they were being slaughtered.

I turned and looked at Diego. *"Dammit!* We need bigger guns!"

Boom!

Boom!

Boom!

I whirled around again. *Cannon fire! When did we get cannons?* Didn't matter, there was a path to the gate!

*

After some "red-shirt" casualties, Diego, his forces, and I managed to beat back the waves of walkers and shut the gates. When the gates were successfully closed it was short work to kill off the walkers in the adjacent area. Eventually the sounds of screams and gunfire were distant and barely audible over the pounding rain. I breathed heavily as bodies lay everywhere.

Some of the blood on the ground had started to clot, but the deluge of rain washed the majority down storm drains. Diego's men worked as best they could to move the bodies out of the way, but there were just too many. Thank god for the rain.

I turned to Diego. "Diego! What the *fuck* happened here? Those gates should have been able to hold those things back!"

Diego looked worried and confused. "I do not know Parker . . . but when we tried to close them we suffered a lightning strike that put a surge through the power system!"

I was shocked. *"What?"*

Diego nodded. *"Sí,* all of the power to man the gates and automated systems were knocked out! I've already sent men to get everything back online."

I stopped and looked around. "Diego, don't you see what's going on!?"

He stopped and looked impatiently at me. "What?"

I waved at the streetlights. "A lightning strike wouldn't have kept the backup generators to the gates from activating." I pointed at the dead walkers. "And look at them! They're still fresh! These things have just recently been infected."

Diego was confused. "I am still having trouble, Parker!"

I jogged to him. "This is a coordinated assault on the fort!"

The color drained from Diego's face before it turned bright red. *"El Fort Montaña no caerá!"*

I didn't understand what he said, so I ignored it. "Diego, calm down, I have a plan!"

Diego looked at me with fury in his eyes. *"¿Qué?"*

"First, we need to push all those walkers off the ledge so they can join their friends at the bottom of the canyon. Second, once they're are on the canyon floor, we cause a massive rock and mud slide to form a giant bowl. When they are corralled into one spot, we fill the bowl with—"

Diego nodded energetically. "We drown them! *¡Perfecto!* I will—"

I grabbed him by the shirt to keep him from taking off. "Diego! That's not it! We need to fill the bowl with the Greek-fire Navarro's been stockpiling!"

Diego was dumbfounded. "How do you know about that?"

I looked him dead in the eyes. "That doesn't matter right now. Have your men get it into the bowl, when the bowl fills, we ignite it. The rain will help the fire to spread and we'll burn them!"

Diego paused. "Impossible! There's no way to activate the formula without being right next to it."

"What about flares or fireworks?"

Diego closed his eyes angrily. "We have none."

I frantically shook my head, trying to think. Then it came to me. "We'll destroy the foundation under the main power transformer in the canyon. When it falls into the bowl it'll send an electrical surge though the water. It'll have a wide enough radius to ignite the fire."

Diego furrowed his brow. "And that will kill them? You are sure this plan will work?"

I shook my head grimly. "No."

"How do we know the fire won't spread to the rest of the mountains? Why don't we just blow up the mountainside and bury them?"

I paused to shoot a walker running at Diego from behind. "Diego, do you know what would happen afterward? If we bury those things in this rain, that mud and rock will become cement and we wouldn't be able to dig them out. In the first week those things will start to rot. Soon after flies will flock here and diseases will run rampant. And while every available hand tries to fruitlessly dig up those bodies, I promise you, the fort will die a slow death. We need to kill them in a way that will make their corpses easily accessible and simple to remove."

Diego frowned. "And how is the Greek fire going to be contained?"

I shook my head. "The rain will wash enough mud and clay down the canyon walls to keep it contained. Eventually it'll burn out!"

Diego paused. "Very well. Where do we start?"

I looked around before looking back at him. "Get the backup generators working so the transformer can generate the needed shock."

Diego nodded. "And then?"

"I need you to divide your men into groups to clear the ledge of the remaining infected, start a mudslide on the cliff-side opposite the transformer, and get the fire in the bowl. When that's finished we'll clear the fort of any more walkers."

Diego and I grasped hands. "Very well, my friend, let us hope this plan works."

I hoped so too.

*

The freezing rain stung my face as I clumsily repelled down an almost vertical drop. The transformer was at least fifty feet from the ground on a slippery, muddy, rocky canyon wall and the only way to it was by rope. But I couldn't dwell on the fact I'm above a canyon filled with crazed cannibals, right now I had to get the dynamite Heloise gave me into position. Still, every fiber of my being was telling me the descent was taking way too long.

My specter appeared next to me. "Of all the stupid things you've done before, this is the third stupidest."

I shook my head and looked for the next foothold. "Shut up."

He whispered into my ear. "No, I'm not going anywhere. I want to be the first to see you fall into the abyss."

I repelled five feet and almost slipped. "I can do this. And I need to concentrate!"

He looked around with a grin. "Then try concentrating on not plummeting into a sea of cannibals."

Even with the man in black whispering in my ear, I finished climbing down the wall and started to prep the explosives and detonator. Simultaneously, Diego would be prepping the cargo tram for its last mission. Diego realized the best way to push the infected into the canyon would be a huge dragnet attached to the tram. The net would then sweep the walkers in. Then the tram will explode at a designated location where it would create the mudslide. That collapse would seal the canyon off at one end and create an enormous bowl that would corral the infected into one area. Once trapped, Diego would release the Greek fire mixture onto the walkers while I sent the transformer into the dark ravine. The power lines containing ten-thousand-plus volts would then ignite the fire and every godforsaken walker would burn. It was also possible the incredible electrical current would course through their hearts and fry their brains, taking out a few before they burned.

My specter appeared next to me. "Of all the stupid things you've done before, this is the third stupidest."

I shook my head and looked for the next foothold. "Shut up."

He whispered into my ear. "No, I'm not going anywhere. I want to be the first to see you fall into the abyss."

I repelled five feet and almost slipped. "I can do this. And I need to concentrate!"

He looked around with a grin. "Then try concentrating on not plummeting into a sea of cannibals."

Even with the man in black whispering in my ear, I finished climbing down the wall and started to prep the explosives and detonator. Simultaneously, Diego would be prepping the cargo tram for its last mission. Diego realized the best way to push the infected into the canyon would be a huge dragnet attached to the tram. The net would then sweep the walkers in. Then the tram will explode at a designated location where it would create the mudslide. That collapse would seal the canyon off at one end and create an enormous bowl that would corral the infected into one area. Once trapped, Diego would release the Greek fire mixture onto the walkers while I sent the transformer into the dark ravine. The power lines containing ten-thousand-plus volts would then ignite the fire and every godforsaken walker would burn. It was also possible the incredible electrical current would course through their hearts and fry their brains, taking out a few before they burned.

I finished putting Heloise's dynamite, plus a little extra Diego gave me, under the cement support that held the transformer. "Done! Time to go."

The phantom stood a few feet away firmly gripping one of the support beams. "Damn . . . how are you going to make it back up?"

I grabbed the rope and started to climb back up the cliff.

He smiled. "You hoping to make it back in time for a hero's welcome?"

When I reached the top I saw the trolley pass by on the other side of the canyon.

He shook his head and faded from view. "Oooo . . . the silent treatment . . . that doesn't bode well."

The tram's lights blared through the heavy rain and it powered through the dark figures of the walkers in its way. Behind it, a giant net swept dozens of monsters into the abyss. I looked on, waiting . . . waiting . . . waiting . . .

The specter looked on with a smile.

Waiting . . . waiting . . .

Booom!

There went the tram . . .

Crash! Rumble! Rumble!

And there went the cliff wall . . .

I waited a few minutes before reaching for the remote detonator. Somewhere along the canyon walls Greek fire was being poured into the ravine. Then one of the flood-lights above the front gate flickered on and turned towards me. Diego was signaling the power had been restored. I hesitated and then braced myself before hitting the switch to the detonator . . .

Boom!

There went the transformer . . .

Zzzzzzzz!

The ravine lit up as more than ten thousand volts ran through the water, shocking the infected while igniting the Greek fire at the same time. I watched as the canyon lit up and an intense fire spread amongst the walkers, burning them to cinders. But before I could enjoy the view I felt my chest seize as the electricity I let loose run through my body. I lost all motor control, fell backwards on the muddy ground, and blacked out.

Chapter 9—To the Hospital

I awoke in the mud as ice cold rain splashed my face.

The man in black looked down on me smugly. "Well . . . you're not dead. How is that?"

My muscles were cramped, my skin wet, and it felt like someone hit my heart with a hammer. I gingerly stood up and glanced down into the burning canyon floor. Every inch was covered in fire and burning bodies. I told Diego the fire would be contained, but I neglected to mention the electricity from the transformer would not. Thankfully I was far enough away that the surge was dispersed enough to not kill me.

The phantom frowned at me. "That was a stupid plan."

"Yup."

I was exhausted. From the climb back up the mountain and the amped-up tazing, I was sore and ready to collapse. But it was probably best to breakdown inside the fort walls. Hopefully no one else was hit by that surge of electricity. Anyone caught in the floodwaters brought on by the rain was in small danger of being tazed . . . like I was. I smiled. Everything that had happened to me would be worth it if the plan worked. If it worked, the walkers outside were all dead and Diego only had to finish up with the remaining ones inside the fort walls.

On the way back the man in black watched me limp up a slope and paused courteously if I slipped or tripped on the slick and rocky ground.

He waited for me to climb over a bolder. "You sure you can make it back to the fort?"

I shook my head. "Can't think about that right now. I just need to focus on putting one foot in front of the other."

When I reached the front gates a feeling of relief swept over me. Uninfected people were pulling and pushing the dead outside, over the edge, and into the ravine.

I sighed. "Wonder how soon the fire will burn itself out?"

I jumped out of my skin as someone behind me yelled my name. "*Parker!*" Diego ran at me with a wide grin but paused as he got a better look at me. "*Díos mío*, Parker. You look as if you fell into that pit with those monsters, are you alright my friend?"

I nodded. "A little extra crispy, but otherwise fine."

He laughed and slapped my already sore back. "Parker! We have won! All of those creatures are destroyed by your brilliant plan—"

I held up a hand. "This isn't over Diego. We need to find the person who opened the gates. This is our only chance of finding out whoever started this."

Diego furrowed his brow. "Bien. You are right, my friend. However, you need to rest. Let my men and me handle this."

I smiled weakly. "I can rest when I'm dead. Oh, and Diego, I've given this some thought . . . but didn't want to bring it up until we dealt with the walkers . . . I think that the Christens might be behind this."

The wrinkles on Diego's forehead deepened as he frowned. "You are sure of this?"

I shook my head. "It is just a feeling, but who else would know how to open the gates? And they have a motive. They might have even enlisted outside help."

Diego looked a little confused. "Why—"

I rolled my eyes. "Revenge. You and your men be sure to double check on Navarro, Alexa, and her husband. They might be—"

Diego's face turned red and he exploded like a volcano. *"¡Esos hijos de puta no va a tocar su!"*

Everyone within fifty feet jumped when Diego let loose his angry roar. His voice was so loud it drowned out the sound of the rain. He turned and ran to the main bunker. But before I could call him back he vanished with several men.

The specter appeared beside me. "Looks like the hothead took off without letting you finish. You were going to suggest sending someone to check on the council members, right?"

I shrugged. "I'm sure he'll get there soon enough. Let's meet him there."

*

I limped up stairs and down hallways to the safety of the council's panic room. But as I reached the hidden entrance I saw the door open and a thought occurred. The Christens have more knowledge of the fort than anyone . . . they would know how and where to get at the council. I held back. I drew my gun and pulled out my knife (I don't know how but I lost my axe somewhere) and slowly walked down the hallway to the ajar door. I drew in a deep breath, prepared my sore and torn muscles for an explosion of energy, and burst into the room.

Then I froze.

The dead bodies of the council members and their families lay strewn across the floor of the panic room. Most looked as if they'd been killed by a shot to the head. The rest were just shot at random with a double-tap to the head.

I tried not to let my emotions erupt. I briefly looked around and then spied the door leading to the outside. That's where the Christens would have made their exit. This way they could kill all the members of the council at once and make their escape. But it looked as if things didn't go according to plan.

Navarro, Alexa, and Matthew weren't here. Navarro would have been the first one they would have killed, Matthew would be the second, and they might have planned to kidnap Alexa. If the Christens wanted the Navarros badly enough, they would have to hunt for them. Then I looked down and spotted a hand axe similar to mine protruding from one of the victims.

I reached down to grab it when I heard Diego bellow my name. *"Parker!"*

Wham!

In less than a second I felt my jaw dislocate as I slammed against the far wall. Things slowed down as I sank to the ground. My weapons clattered to the floor and slid across the floor. I tried to look around, but it was too disorienting trying to look through the blood pooling in the eye that hit the wall. Eventually I managed to push the pain to the back of my mind long enough to see three struggling blurs across the room and one take a defensive position over me. They were protecting me *from* Diego.

I heard him yell as my head spun. *"Parker! ¿Qué has hecho aquí?"*

I blinked the blood from my eye and motioned to the man between me and Diego. After spitting as much blood from my mouth as possible, I wheezed a message into his ear.

The man knelt beside me and looked at Diego as he translated my words. "He says it was the Christens and they escaped through the door."

Diego froze and looked around the room. Other men nodded, telling Diego I was right. The information sank in and a horrified look came over Diego.

Through a shamed voice he whispered. "I am so sorry, my friend."

Then Diego and some of his men left . . . no doubt trying to catch up with the traitors. Then my vision got hazy and I passed out.

*

A gun fired and something collapsed next to me, and then I heard an old woman's voice and several boots run out the escape door. "Come on, we don't have time for this! They will be here any second!"

A louder, angrier voice rang in my ears. *"No!* I want this bastard!"

After a few frustrated clicks I saw a gun fall to the ground beside me. I felt my body move. I was numb, so I could only assume someone was kicking me in my stomach because they couldn't shoot me.

The first person yelled at the second in a rapid and hushed voice. "Charles Christen! We can't stay! They already have your uncle!"

Through waves of pain and numbness, I felt a deepening panic wriggle through my bruised and possibly hemorrhaging internal organs. I tried looking around the room, but my eyes were clouded with blood.

The first voice spoke rapidly. "Unless you have forgotten, you have used up all our bullets, left your knife in that slut Alexa, and Diego is going to be—did you hear that? Christ! They're here! Charlie, we need to leave *now*!"

Charlie shook me by my wet and muddy shirt frantically looking for a weapon. "Fine . . . this isn't the last you'll hear from me!"

And with a final stomp to my face, the two blobs ran into the dark passageway. Then I passed out once again, choking on my blood.

*

Crack!

"Ahhhhhhhhhhhhhhhhhhhhh!" I woke up screaming as every inch of my body convulsed in pain. My jaw throbbed as it was relocated. Through unfocused eyes I saw a blob gently caress my cheek before putting weight on my chest while a different blob moved toward my shoulder . . .

Snap!

"Aaaaaahhhhhhhhhhhhhhhhhh!!!"

*

Dark . . . I can't see anything. Oh, it's night? For a moment I thought . . .

*

Light . . . it's morning? I'm awake? Where am?

*

Dark . . . I think it's night again . . . I feel much better . . . and judging from that . . . that . . . strangely articulated sentence, I think . . . I don't have . . . brain damage. Huh, my nose itch—

"Aaaaahhh!" I yelled as the pain overtook me and I passed out again.

*

Passed out again . . . I hurt so much . . . I guess if I can feel pain it means I'm not paralyzed . . . or dead. Let's see . . . there's a bandage on my nose . . . guess someone broke it . . . my . . . my ribs ache . . . hope they didn't . . . puncture a lung . . . and . . . and my left arm and right leg are . . . are in pretty heavy casts . . . they must have been broken too. *Wow . . . that is a huge bandage on my stomach* . . . there's a bloodstain in it. Crap . . . I must have had some . . . internal damage . . . for them to . . . to oper . . . operate on me . . . like this . . . What hap—? . . . *Diego . . . god . . . damn . . . Die—*

*

I angrily glared at a painted white ceiling as I yelled at someone. "He is reason I'm in the sorry shape I'm in! Goddamn him!"

I didn't know who I was talking to. I hadn't been able to think very well with the throbbing pain in my head, but whomever I was yelling at seemed less inclined to stay with me.

The voice started to crack. "But he is so sorry . . . and when he saw you in the room with all those dead bodies he assumed the worst and . . . and just lost control . . ."

I tried looking away, but the neck brace wouldn't let me. "*Go* away . . ."

Whomever it was tried stepping into my line of sight. "But isn't he your best—"

I glared at a grayish blob. "*Go . . . away . . .*"

The blob backed off and whispered, "Okay."

*

It had been a full month since the attack and since Diego put me in the hospital. Charlie might have broken my body, but Diego made it possible for him to do it. I still couldn't move my neck due to whiplash. My arms and legs were weighed down by heavy and immobilizing casts. It also hurt to breathe or move because my sternum and eight of my ribs were cracked or severely bruised. I was also healing from major surgeries inside my abdomen. At least I didn't pass out today, and I was a little recognizable. Good thing the information concerning medical advancements survived the end of the world.

A dark figure sat in a chair across the room. "Boy, aren't you in a sorry state?"

I frowned and looked at the immobile ceiling fan. "Yeah, well, I had some help."

He smiled his wry smile. "I wonder when we can—"

A good-looking, if a little unkempt, nurse interrupted my phantom as she poked her head inside the room. "I'm sorry to bother you, Mr. Parker, but I thought I heard you speaking to someone."

I looked at her from the corner of my eye. "No problem, Holly. But I do have a favor to ask you . . ."

She smiled "Yes?"

I looked at the fan. "I'd like the ceiling fan on if possible."

She looked at me with an apologetic expression and opened a window instead. "Sorry, but we are on a limited supply of power and need to conserve energy."

I smiled at the ceiling fan. "How long until the power supply is on again?"

She gave me an exaggerated shrug. "I don't know, but almost everyone is working to set up the new transformer since *someone* destroyed the last one."

I flinched as I tried to grin. "I don't think I like the way you're rolling your eyes at me."

She smiled and excused herself. Ever since I woke up, Holly was practically the only person who spent any time with me. Alexa occasionally limped by for check-ups and would sometimes ask if I will like to see Diego because he'd like very much to see me. I said *no* as politely and with as much restraint as I could muster. Afterward she'd weakly smile, get a little teary eyed, and excuse herself before she did anything embarrassing. I refused all other visitors. I didn't want anyone to see me like this.

Except for Heloise. She managed to force her way in. She was more than interested in hearing about the events of the attack, but even that conversation drifted to what we'd been doing since and things we might do after I healed. Midway through she locked the door, pulled out an old iPod with small speakers, and pulled me into a fantastic kiss before starting to shake her hips to the songs as she put on a little soft-core strip show.

I *really* wished I could move.

*

I sat in a wheelchair in the shade of a pretty tree. "Hugh. Bored, bored, bored, bored . . ."

Holly approached me from behind. "Um, Mr. Parker?"

I looked straight ahead as I chanted my new mantra. "Bored, bored, bored, bored, bored, bored, bored, bored . . ."

She tapped my shoulder as I continued the word of the day. "Mr. Parker?"

It had been around two months since I'd been in the hospital. I really couldn't remember because I'd left my sense of time on the floor of the old safe room. I was bored because I couldn't do very much because I *still* had most of my casts on. It really shouldn't take this long to heal. It was as if they were intentionally keeping me in the hospital. Still . . . at least I was out of my room, and the aids wheeled me to a pretty garden with a great view of the fort.

Holly tapped my shoulder again. "Mr. Parker."

I enjoyed the green grass, oak saplings, blue sky, and rich sun. Ever since the storm put water in the dried soil, the plants and crops have flourished. I was starting to enjoy the quiet, until Holly came along with an uninvited and unwanted visitor.

My neck was still stiff, but I turned my head slightly toward her. "Holly, I heard you. I may still be in recovery from major head trauma, but that doesn't mean I've lost my hearing."

She stepped into my line of sight. "Mr. Diego has come to see you. I tried to turn him away, but he is determined to see you."

I turned my head away from her. "Try again."

She leaned back into my sight line. "Pardon?"

I sorely turned and frowned at her. "Turn him away again."

She looked back regretfully. "I'm sorry, but he's—"

In a tentative voice I heard my name. "Parker . . ."

I painfully craned my neck and looked at Diego. This was the first time I saw him since he sucker-punched me and left me on the ground so Charlie could beat the living tar out of me. He was hunched over and wore an ashamed expression.

I turned my head back to the courtyard. "Say what you need to say, Diego."

He stepped forward. "Parker . . . esta *duro*—ah . . . it's hard for me to say, *pero yo soy tris*—ah! I mean . . . I am sorry . . ."

I continued to stare at him. "Diego, it has been hard for me too . . . it's been hard to breathe, move, and even stay conscious for long periods of time. Ever since you left me on the floor, leaving me helpless for Charlie to punch, and kick, and pound the *shit* out—"

He took another step forward and raised his hands in frustration. "That wasn't my fault—"

I flinched as I glared at him. "Like *hell* it wasn't!"

He looked at me in dismay. "I swear I was not thinking clearly, I—"

I hit the armrest of the wheelchair with my good arm. "*Goddammit, Diego!* I thought you, above all, would have the integrity to take responsibility for the events your actions put in motion."

He paused and looked away.

I looked away too. "Perhaps you should leave."

He looked up and spoke in a quiet voice "No . . ."

I winced again as I glance at him in anger. *"What?"*

Diego walked into my line of sight with arms spread out as a gesture of peace. "Parker, you are right. I acted too rashly and you suffered because of it. If I was given the chance I would stop myself. No words or actions can make up for the wrongs I did to you. My friend . . . I am begging you . . . please forgive me."

My heart continued to race as my rage kept building.

I wanted to scream at him to leave. But . . . that was not the right thing to do. I paused a moment to breathe the fire out of my lungs and inhale clean and cool air. My mind briefly drifted back to the last scene in the 1942 film *Casablanca* with Humphrey Bogart and Ingrid Bergman. Bogart was giving his heartfelt speech of how one day regret will come to all those who do not do the right thing. "If that plane leaves the ground and you're not on it, you'll regret it. Maybe not today. Maybe not tomorrow. But soon and for the rest of your life." I closed my eyes, *If I do not forgive Diego here and now, I will regret it.*

I sighed and looked at him wearily. "Diego . . . I accept your apology."

He weakly smiled. "Thank you, my friend."

I leaned back. "Please . . . let me be alone for now . . . I am really tired."

Out of the corner of my eye I watched Diego leave in a more relieved posture than when he arrived.

Holly stepped in front of me. "I am very proud of you."

I halfheartedly smiled. "Holly, I want you to leave too."

She looked confused for a moment. "O-okay . . ."

She turned and followed Diego.

Why is forgiveness so damn tiring?

When they were both gone, the man in black stepped out of the shadows. "I'm not so proud you. I think things were more—"

I glowered at him. "Go away. I am too tired to talk with you."

He grinned wolfishly. "Well . . . just because you asked so nice."

*

It had been roughly two weeks since Diego came to beg for forgiveness, and I decided it was time to let everyone else see me. Alexa and her husband were the first to visit. Alexa was so overcome with emotion that she started crying while thanking me. She said Diego hadn't been the same man since he thrashed me but he became his old self after I forgave him. Tiffany and her sisters came as soon as their young legs could carry them to give their love. Various other people stopped by, many saying they were on the grounds the night of the attack and I saved their lives. Eventually it all became too much, and I started refusing visitors just to be at peace. But one visitor muscled her way in.

Heloise took a small break from the power station to come see me. Apparently she was a little disappointed I forgave Diego. She loved seeing the usually overly energetic Diego sulk and twist in the wind whenever she mentioned my name.

I smiled at her. "You don't really mean that, Heloise."

She folded her arms and rolled her eyes. "I don't know, Parker. He stayed out of my way and off my nerves when he had that dark cloud of guilt hanging over his head. Now it seems a wave of emotions burst through a dam. Now he's more annoying than before."

She plopped down on my bed, dangerously close to a very tender rib, but something told me she knew that.

I smiled and winced. "You are too cruel."

With a devilish smile and a light crinkle of her nose, Heloise leaned in closer and gave me a light kiss. But before I could kiss her back, she said, "No, you aren't getting any more than that until you can stand up in a shower—and you could really use one. Plus, don't you dare think I'm just being a tease. Instead . . . think of me as your motivation to get out of this dreary hospital room."

Before I could reply, she slipped out of my room in such a cool and fluid motion that she could have been a stream of water from the last rain. I never felt so damned frustrated with my bandages and casts than at that moment.

Chapter 10—Out of the Hospital

Heloise sounded offended when I asked her to come see me. "So what do you want me to do, drop what I'm doing just for you?"

I was a little let down. "Heloise, I am getting out of the hospital today, and I would really like to see you."

"Parker, just because I have a special interest in you doesn't mean I am going to make you a priority. I did not become director of power operations from being touchy-feely."

I halfheartedly laughed. "Sexy, smart, and driven."

She grinned over the line. "You bet your ass."

I sighed and rubbed my eyes. "So you're sure you can't take time off to come see me?"

She spoke in a huff. "No. Didn't you hear what I just said? *I did not* become director of operations from being touchy—" And then, to someone else: "Yes, what is it? I told you I was in an important meeting . . . he did what! Oh, I am so firing that man!" And then back to Parker: "I'm sorry, but I need to fire someone."

I ran my fingers through my hair. "Okay see you"—click—"around."

She hung up on me. God I loved that woman. Of course it was still too soon to tell her that; her pride and fear of commitment would most definitely make her turn me away. Oh well, things would work out sooner or later. I'd wait.

I hung up and Holly walked in with a wide stride. "Mr. Parker, it's time to get you out of here."

I smiled at her. "Ahhh, Holly, it is a pleasure to see you."

She smiled back. "Okay, you can turn off the flattering prince-charming thing . . ."

I shrugged. "You're right. I'm sure my envious Heloise would not appreciate that."

She stiffened a little. "You know . . . I wasn't supposed to tell you this . . . but last time Heloise visited, she overheard us gossiping about you and told us you were forbidden territory. She even said if she ever caught us putting the moves on you, or even heard we tried, she would drive us out into the middle of the desert and leave us to die a slow and painful death from dehydration."

I smiled as I pulled off the hospital gown when she handed me new clothes. "Ah, she's a real peach, isn't she?"

Holly closed her eyes, put a hand on her forehead, and sighed. "I will never understand men and their obsession with bad girls. She's a freakin' succubus, Parker."

I nodded. "Yeah, ahhh . . . what's a succubus?"

She turned to me with a sullen face. "You need to read more. A succubus is a female demon that drains the life out of men who fall for her beauty."

I smiled. "Sounds like a normal relationship to me."

Holly frowned at me and shook her head.

I raised my hands apologetically. "Kidding! I was just kidding. Holly, you need to lighten up."

She scowled at me, and with a pout she left to get a wheelchair while I continued dressing.

She paused before leaving the room. "You shouldn't be with her."

I sat on the bed after putting my belt on and started buttoning my blue-gray shirt. I paused and looked down at my flabby stomach. Hmmm . . . I seriously needed to hit the gym.

The phantom stepped from the shadows with his habitual grin. "I have to give you props, Parker, I didn't realize you could be so cold. Especially to that cute little number."

I didn't look at him. "Holly is just a girl with a small case of Florence Nightingale syndrome. She will be fine as soon as a cute boy her age comes in and sweeps her off her feet."

The phantom cocked an eyebrow. "And I thought *I* was supposed to be the ruthless one."

I sighed. "All's fair in love and war."

After roughly five months I was finally being shown out of the hospital by way of wheelchair. I was free of all casts, restraints, poor cooking, and . . . and . . . well, the point was, I received a clean bill of health. And when all the good-byes were out of the way, I planned to tour the fort and see the headway on the reconstruction. The fort was in pretty sorry shape after what was unofficially deemed "the Charlie Incident," and from what I'd heard, progress was slow. But as I was bidding farewell to the medical staff, I found myself looking directly into a pair of sharp, sapphire-blue eyes.

Heloise had sneaked up behind me. "Parker . . . it has been ages . . . my god, you need to work out. Well, the first thing we are going to do is renew your gym membership."

"My god I missed you."

She brushed me off like dandruff. "Of course you did. Now come here."

She grabbed me by the collar of my new shirt and pulled me into a passionate kiss that seemed to last a lifetime. I wished it could have gone on longer.

*

I began to regret being so enthusiastic about leaving the hospital. As soon as our passionate reunion ended, Heloise did exactly what she promised—she dragged me straight to a gym—and it wasn't long before I figured out she was going to be a slave driver. For four weeks she put me through every damn workout routine ever recorded in a fitness book, during which time she made me wear heavier and heavier weights under my clothing. That meant wearing weights during the insanely long laps through the fort and during the workout routines. Still, that wasn't the worst part—that was when she restricted my diet to only the boring and healthy foods while pulling anything tasty out of reach. All the while she kept repeating, "If you want a wild night with me, you'd better shape up."

Take today for example . . . she woke me up at the crack of dawn and fixed me a bland breakfast of two eggs, one-half glass of milk, unbuttered, untoasted whole wheat bread, and one apple.

As I looked at the meal with disinterest, she smiled back. "Parker, once you are finished with you meal, change for your fifteen-mile run. Then you are going to do your regular routine, except . . . let's add another dozen or so sit-ups and pushups today."

I rubbed my forehead. "Greeeeaaa—"

I stopped mid-sarcastic remark as Heloise narrowed her eyes. "Right . . . thirty miles it is . . . I think I'm done here."

She smiled and began to eat. "I put your sweats through the laundry. They are now on your bed."

I let out an exasperated sigh. "Thank you."

She giggled and replied, "You're welcome."

The way she sat there, smiling . . . she might as well have told me that we were going for a walk in the park. I shook my head and thought about her routine compared to mine. When she was ready, she would change and run with me for about five miles before leaving for a light workout at the council members' private gym, go back to my place for a shower, and then wait for me at the gym to monitor my routine.

I let out another sigh.

I turned the lights on as I entered my room, and sure enough the sweats were on the bed. I stripped and thought about playing hooky as I held my pants up . . . and then a cold shiver ran up my spine as I remembered the last time I tried to skip out on a workout. The nurses at the hospital were perfectly correct to be anxious around Heloise. And, as if on cue, she walked into my room. She watched me . . . actually, she was probably judging my progress. It had been four weeks, but the workout goal wasn't a target weight, it was an examination. Heloise said I could stop my vigorous routine when I had the body of a twenty-year-old and I make her knees weak when she saw my butt.

I finished dressing and started on my way out. "All right I'm off. You coming?"

She smiled and lightly shook her head. "Hmmm? Oh . . . not today."

I smiled back and turned to put my pajamas away. "All right, see you later. Love you."

We both froze. I glanced back at her only to see her black hair disappear into the hallway. Two seconds later I heard the front door of my apartment slam.

Wait! What did I just do? Holy crap I—I—*said it.* I didn't mean to; it just slipped out . . . crap.

*

I ran the thirty miles as fast as I possibly could, feebly hoping Heloise would be waiting at the gym. She wasn't today. A pit formed in my stomach, and I started to feel incredibly weak. I knew what I did was a really stupid . . . what if it was too early to say that? She might . . .

Wham!

Out of nowhere something fast knocked me to the ground and fell on top me.

Ouch! What the hell did I run into? "Heloise?"

I looked up and Heloise looked back at me.

"Heloise! Are you okay?"

She grabbed me by the face and pulled me into the most forceful kiss I ever experienced. When we finally came up for air, her hair fell around us, cutting us off from the rest of the world. She looked at me in a way that was far different from the sarcastic, cool, and composed expression she usually had.

She had trouble putting words together. "I . . . Parker . . . I, I don't know."

I put my arms around her and hugged her tightly. "I love you too, Heloise."

Then we ran back to my apartment and made love. We had no other choice. What else could we do?

*

Normally Heloise would shower after sex and sometimes say it was great and that she couldn't wait until next time, but now . . . we actually held each other. We laid together and talked about things we avoided before. I told her how my memory was spotty, how a dark figure from my past haunts me whenever I'm left alone, and how he taunts me by dangling answers to questions in front of me.

However, my story didn't compare to her dark epic.

She talked about how her mother abandoned her to foster care when she was six and after years of frustrating and guilty confusion she learned her mother was actually trying to hide from her dangerous father. She then talked about school and how she couldn't connect with her peers because she was so smart and insecure. But the worst chapter started when she graduated high school. Like a Shakespearean tragedy, everything started perfectly. She was accepted by one of the top universities in the country, she made friends, she became closer to her foster family, and she even married the perfect man.

Mark was tall, handsome, well built, witty, kind, and great at sex . . . but it soon became apparent those things were superficial. It started when he pressed her to drop out of college, become a housewife, and then become a stay-at-home mother. When she refused, he pressed harder and harder while becoming angrier after every refusal. Eventually he started throwing tantrums by yelling, punching holes through walls, and breaking dishes. She tried to stand her ground, thinking things would get better over time, but when he became violent and hit her, she had enough and left him.

Several weeks after she filed for divorce she discovered the depths of his relentlessness. He made countless phone calls, sent presents, and tried to meet with her to "explain" what happened and apologize. It became so bad she filed a restraining order, but that was just the prelude to a month-long journey through an inferno. He started sending threats over the phone and through the mail to her, her friends, and her family. Two weeks after that he posted private nude photos of her on the walls of their university and put up sex tapes of her on the Internet. But it didn't end there. On the third week he snatched her as she was getting out of her car. For two weeks he held her captive, tied up in a hole in the floor under the living room couch.

She managed to escape by dislocating her arm and breaking the hinge to the trap door. She then resolved to end everything once and for all. She waited until he got home, and using his shotgun she shot off his testicles, his kneecaps, and finally his head.

After she finished her story, she sat up and pulled her hair away from her back and revealed a huge burn scar at the base of her hairline. She said she had a doctor burn that patch of skin to hide another branded scar in the shape of an *M*.

I couldn't imagine the depths of hate in that man's heart until I saw the scar. With that branding iron he labeled her as a thing and not a person. Even though the letter was gone, that little patch of blemished skin would serve as a reminder of her humiliation at the hands of that bastard for the rest of her life.

Damn him.

She asked me if I felt any different about her, but I felt such a mixture of rage, sorrow, and regret that I couldn't say anything. So I just held her close, kissed her, and wiped the makeup running down her face.

It wasn't a surprise when Heloise was gone when I woke the following morning. She might not have been ready to confront her past, and I'm sure it was ten times harder to tell me. When I looked around, I spotted a note left on the kitchen countertop.

Parker,

I need some time to figure some things out. Don't contact me. Please wait for me. I'll be in contact with you soon. I love you.

PS: Stay in shape.

About the Author

Casey Johnston is a college student who hopes his part-time hobby will bear fruit. At least he hopes that he can make back the rediculous amount of money he spent on having his first book published. He uses information gathered from zombie fan sites and reputable source material to hash together his first book. A book loosely based on a dream which was later turned into a highschool literature project that got an A- for PG-13 crass language.